A Winter Book

SELECTED STORIES

Sort Of
BOOKS

A Winter Book

Selected Stories

Tove Jansson

*Translated from the Swedish by
Silvester Mazzarella, David McDuff
and Kingsley Hart*

Introduced by
Ali Smith

Published in 2006 by Sort Of Books, PO Box 18678, London NW3 2FL

Distributed by the Penguin Group in all territories
excluding the United States and Canada:
Penguin Books, 80 Strand, London WC2R 0RL

Typeset in Goudy and GillSans to a design by Henry Iles
Printed in Italy by L.E.G.O. S.p.A.
208pp
A catalogue record for this book is available from the British Library
ISBN 0-9548995-2-0 EAN 9780954899523

Thanks

Sort Of thanks, above all, Sophia Jansson, Helen Svensson of Schildts, and Ali Smith, for their help in compiling and selecting this edition; and Silvester Mazzarella, Kingsley Hart and David McDuff for their luminous translations. We are also very grateful for the contributions and enthusiasm of Philip Pullman, Frank Cottrell Boyce and Esther Freud; to Erja Sandell, Peter Dyer, Henry Iles, Miranda Davies, Tim Chester and Adele Baviera for production; and Holly Marriott and Jason Craig at Penguin.

Special thanks also to Hildi Hawkins from *Books from Finland*, who first published the translations of *Messages* and *Taking Leave*. www.finlit.fi/booksfromfinland

Photos used in the book

Inside covers:
Tove Jansson by mast © Lars Jansson.
Summer Island under snow © Per-Olov Jansson.
Tove Jansson in coat © Alf Lidman.
Tove Jansson and Tuulikki Pietilä with kite, Tove drawing with her
mother, Ham (Signe Hammarsten Jansson), and Studio of Viktor
Jansson (Tove's father) © Jansson Family archive.

Inside Images:
p.1, p.10, p. 71, p. 80, p. 101, p. 203, p. 208 © Per Olov Jansson.
p.8 (Tove Jansson), p.19 (Viktor Jansson), p.29 (Tove Jansson),
p.45 (Tove and Ham), p.55 (Viktor and Poppolino), p.60 (Viktor in
studio), p.95 (Viktor and Ham in boat), p.110 (Tove Jansson), p.125
(Tove Jansson and Tuulikki Pietilä) © Jansson Family archive.
p.132 © Len Waernberg.
p.154 © Margareta Strömstedt.
p.186 © Alf Lidman.

Original publications and their translations

The Stone; Parties; The Dark; Snow; German Measles; Flying; Annie; The Iceberg; Albert; Flotsam and Jetsam; High Water; Jeremiah; The Spinster Who Had An Idea. All from *The Sculptor's Daughter (Bildhuggarens dotter)*, Schildts Förlags Ab, 1968. First published in English by Ernest Benn Ltd, 1969. Translated by Kingsley Hart, 1969.

The Boat and Me; Messages. From *Meddelande: Noveller I Urval 1971–97*, Schildts Förlags Ab, 1998. Translated by Silvester Mazzarella, 2005, 2001.

The Squirrel. From *Lyssnerskan*, Schildts Förlags Ab, 1971. Translated by Silvester Mazzarella, 2005.

Letters from Klara. From *Brev fran Klara*, Schildts Förlags Ab, 1991. Translated by Silvester Mazzarella, 2006.

Correspondence; Travelling Light. From *Resa med lätt bagage*, Schildts Förlags Ab, 1987. Translated by Silvester Mazzarella, 2005.

Taking Leave (an extract). From *Anteckningar från en ö*, Schildts Förlags Ab, 1996. Translated by David McDuff, 1996.

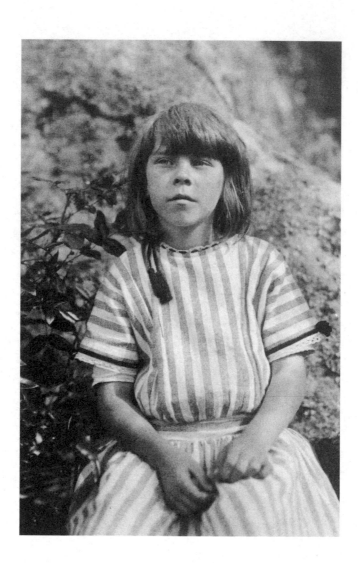

Contents

Introduction

by Ali Smith

"How old must you be to write a story?" a young Japanese fan wrote and asked her heroine, the Finnish writer and illustrator Tove Jansson. Jansson, at this point, was in her seventies and world-famous as the creator and illustrator of the Moomins, the extended family of big-nosed philosophising creatures (and their various neighbours, including a tiny anarchist no bigger than a thumbnail) who, simply by mildness and geniality, survive the terrible upheavals of their often topsy-turvy life in a beautiful Scandinavian setting of mountains, forests, seas and valleys.

Jansson was then – and is now – much less well known for her fiction for adults, which she began to write in her early fifties and which she concentrated on for over three decades, pretty much the rest of her life (she died in 2001 at the age of 86). Typically, she kept that Japanese girl's beautiful, spare letters and, as if to demonstrate that art can sometimes be what life itself sends you, but delivered back to you through clearer eyes, she transformed them into 'Correspondence', a miraculously lightly held short story about youth and age, connection and isolation, published here in English for the first time.

In fact, this collection is the first selection of Jansson's short fiction for adults to be published in an English translation for nearly forty years. The recent UK reprint of her classic 1972 novel *The Summer Book*, thirty years after its original publication, has done a lot to remind readers that the brilliance, the thoughtful originality and the blithe hilarious anarchy people associate with her tales of Moominvalley are really only half the story of Jansson's quiet creative genius. Her ten books of fiction for adults – her novels, short story collections and memoir writing – form an equally shining achievement.

A Winter Book has been selected to provide as full a view as possible of Jansson's short story work, with an array of pieces hard to find in English, and collected here for the first time in the book's final section. The book also comprises some of the choicest stories from her very first collection, *Sculptor's Daughter* (*Bildhuggarens dotter*, 1968), which she published when she was 54. *Sculptor's Daughter*, one of her most dynamic works, was her first book written specifically for adults rather than children and, interestingly, its subject is childhood itself. Its gloriously funny, disarming and charming set of semi-autobiographical stories of a small girl wintering in Helsinki and summering on a small Finnish island haven't been available in English since 1969.

Beautifully crafted and deceptively simple-seeming, these stories are like pieces of scattered light. In their suppleness, their childlike wilfulness, they're much less melancholy than the average Moomin tale. Light-footed, skilful and mischievous, they belie both the age of their writer, a woman in her middle years, and the fact that they were written in the stark afterlight of her mother's old age and ten years after her father's death.

Jansson grew up a bohemian artistic child, a daughter of artists and bohemians; her mother was the famous Finnish/ Swedish illustrator and artist Signe Hammarsten; her father, Viktor Jansson, was an equally well-known sculptor; and if the very notion of the creative family resides at the centre of Moomin-lore, then these short stories – partly autobiographical, though always wholly crafted into story in their own right – give renewed meaning to words like 'creative' and 'family'. After her mother's death in 1970 she would write her last book for children, *Moominvalley in November*; she followed this with *The Summer Book*, her acknowledged adult masterpiece: the simple, spare story of a very old woman and a very young girl and the adventures, losses and gains there inevitably are when great age and youth live together on a very small Scandinavian island for the whole of an endlessly lit summer.

But Jansson's short stories are as yet unacknowledged small masterworks. Each is distilled to an essence. "You should never keep a single inessential object in your boat," as the adventuring girl tells herself and us at the beginning of 'The Boat and Me'. These are stories that could safely weather storms; they're written with the kind of economy that makes a story rich, and with the kind of precision that turns any mere clockwork of narrative into something that goes beyond time itself.

Parts I and *II* are stories originally from *Sculptor's Daughter*, rearranged here seasonally into winter stories (*Snow*), then summer stories (*Flotsam and Jetsam*). The winter stories are largely town-based and the summer ones island-and-sea stories, a landscape that readers of *The Summer Book* will immediately recognise. Jansson herself spent every summer living and working on a tiny island off the coast of Finland with her lifelong partner, the graphic artist Tuulikki Pietilä; as winter drew in, they would return to their shared flats in Helsinki, and one of the finest pieces here is the collection's final one, the beautiful and honest 'Taking Leave', which records the end of their island life, an end enforced by their own old age. Its perfect final image of release allows this collection to end on what you might call a real high.

So *A Winter Book* modulates between winter and summer, youth and old age. 'The Boat and Me' – a story which seems as if it should have been part of, but has somehow cast itself out on its headstrong own journey away from, the safer moorings of *Sculptor's Daughter* – was also published when Jansson was in her eighties. It is included here as a go-between story before the final part– *Travelling Light* – whose theme is maturity and whose stories, all written when she was between her sixties and eighties, have been selected from various collections and sources to give a taste of Jansson's artful, often funny and always spellbinding take on the hardships and release of later life. Three of her stories on the subject of writing letters have also been brought together for the first time, and some of her more obviously autobiographical writing here reveals some of the hilarious nonsense and ephemera which fame brought her in old age, as well as exposing something a little closer to existential.

What? Scandinavia and existentialism? Don't expect the heavy old, dark old cliché. Though they never miss a challenge, though they're very much about the dark, about risk, violence, jealousy, fears of abandonment, and though they never short-change a reader when it comes to the truth about anything unsettling, these stories are the opposite of heavy. Whether they're about crabbed age or youth, they make an art of lightness, of letting go.

Take one of the later stories, 'The Squirrel', where an old woman living on an island becomes fixated by the visit of a far-too-unreliable wild creature. The story's refrain is the word 'grey' and its subject is the process of growing old. But its protagonist, in her well-meaningness and her determination, shares a lot with the child protagonist of the stories in *Sculptor's Daughter*. Though it reads as more realistically shocked, numbed out of the confidence, the trusting innocence, of the child-stories, it shares with them the same fascination with the fight between existential release and optimistic disgruntlement, or force of will, as can be found in a story like 'The Iceberg'. Here the child, excited by seeing a perfectly formed tiny iceberg, decides to jump into it and sail away in its grotto like mouth. But the iceberg is just too far out of reach. "It was lying there bumping against the rocks at the end of the point where it was deep, and there was deep black water and just the wrong distance between us. If it had been shorter I should have jumped over; if it had been a little longer I could have thought: What a pity, no one can manage to get over that." Instead, she throws her lit torch into it. Then she watches it float away, all lit up, triumphant. It's beautiful. The child wonders how long the batteries will last. Then she despises herself for not risking the jump.

This glorious creation of a child-self, with all her cowardice, her jealousies, her funniness, her witty wilfulness, her precocious understanding of the mechanics of art and her unprejudiced filtering of the adult wisdoms fed to her, is the perfect literary voice. It is innocent, and is all about inference and the getting of knowledge. It is as if the stories themselves are saying, just like the child does: "I know. I know a lot that I don't talk about." They explore human urges at base. They examine the creative urge and the destructive urge. They get very close to real violence and anger. They are always revealingly aware – via the child's blithe innocence, her very unawareness – of class and gender prejudices.

These slight-seeming stories are really discrete philosophical gifts. 'Flying' is directly about lightness, the flight of the imagination, yes, and about the imaginative act of shaking off individual guilt – but in the end this story, in whose finale the whole of Helsinki (including "cats and dogs and guinea-pigs and monkeys" as well as the President) takes to the sky, banishes northern work ethic and shows how creative power has to be hand-in-hand with generosity if it's going to get anything off the ground. 'The Stone', a diminutive reworking of the myth of Sisyphus, is enthralled by what looks weighty. Its child-self battles to roll all the way home, and then up some impossible stairs a stone as big as herself and much, much heavier, which she has decided is a massive lump of precious metal. This story, about the real worth of things, shows how richness is found in the least likely places as well as how everything ordinary becomes silvered-over by adventure – even adventure that ends in what looks like abject failure. The noise the stone makes as it falls down through the building means "Every door opened and everybody ran up and down the stairs". It's a story that goes out of its way to make shut doors open.

The fact that the stories are so brief somehow suggests an eternity, a complete world. It is an extraordinary feat. With a child's pure adamance, Jansson, the laureate of small things, is confident of the value in the seemingly worthless. The *Sculptor's Daughter* stories are held between present and past tense in a way that creates a new kind of time, at once vital, happening right now, and yet safely past, preserved in memory. They make, with a double-edged consciousness that's often very funny, a space that's neither simply adult nor childlike but is somehow believably both. An innocence in these stories puts the innocence back into adulthood, yet preserves the potential and knowing space that childhood is.

A *Winter Book* is full of stories that make art of life and celebrate the life of art. In the process, and like everything Tove Jansson wrote, they celebrate the endless, unstoppable, good-natured force of the imagination. They take, for instance, the attempts to communicate, the blunt requests, the repeated language-stammers of a total stranger, that Japanese girl fan, and, in a typical Jansson combination of inference and clear-sightedness, reveal them as a beautiful story in their own right, a fine tight-roped balance of hope and hopelessness. The stories face age, youth, and each of the dark and light seasons with the same determination to make something light of it all. In their slightness they may seem almost dismissible, but they light up the dark for miles like that torch drifting away on the unmoored iceberg: "Perhaps that torch would go on shining at the bottom of the sea after the iceberg had melted and turned into water." These small acts of seeming accident and covert deliberation make something momentous happen.

PART I

Snow

The Stone

IT WAS LYING BETWEEN THE COAL DUMP AND THE GOODS wagons under some bits of wood and it was a miracle that no one had found it before me. The whole of one side shone with silver and if you rubbed away the coal dust you could see that the silver was there inside the stone too. It was a huge stone of nothing but silver, and no one had found it.

I didn't dare to hide it; somebody might see it and take it while I ran home. It had to be rolled away. If anyone came and tried to stop me I would sit down on the stone and yell my head off. I could bite them as they tried to lift it. I could do just anything.

And so I began to roll it. It was very slow work. The stone just lay on its back quite still, and when I got it to turn over it just lay on its tummy and rocked to and fro. The silver came off in thin flakes that stuck to the ground and broke into small pieces when I tried to pick them up.

I got down on my knees to roll it, which was much better. But the stone only moved half a turn at a time and it was terribly slow work. No one took any notice of me as long as I was rolling down in the harbour. Then I managed to get the stone onto a pavement and things became more difficult. People stopped and tapped on the pavement with their umbrellas and said all sorts of things. I said nothing and just looked at their shoes. I pulled my woolly hat down over my eyes and just went on rolling and rolling and rolling and then the stone had to cross the road. By then I had been rolling it for hours and I hadn't looked up once and hadn't listened to anything anyone said to me. I just gazed at the silver underneath all the coal dust and other dirt and made a tiny little room for myself where nothing existed except the stone and me. But now it had to cross the road.

One car after another went past and sometimes a tram, and the longer I waited, the more difficult it was to roll the stone out into the road.

In the end I began to feel weak at the knees and then I knew that soon it would be too late, in a few seconds it would be too late, so I let it fall into the gutter and began rolling very quickly and without looking up. I kept my nose just above the top of the stone so that the room I had hidden us in would be as tiny as possible and I heard very clearly how all the cars stopped and were angry, but I drew a line between them and me and just went on rolling and rolling. You can close your mind to things if something is important enough. It works very well. You make yourself very small, shut your eyes tight and say a big word over and over again until you're safe.

When I got to the tram-lines I felt tired, so I lay across the stone and held it tight. But the tram just rang and rang its bell so I had to start rolling again, but now I wasn't scared any longer, just angry and that felt much better. Anyway, the stone and I had such a tiny room for ourselves that it didn't matter a bit who shouted at us or what they shouted. We felt terribly strong. We had no trouble in getting onto the pavement again and we continued up the slope to Wharf Road, leaving behind us a narrow trail of silver. From time to time we stopped to rest together and then we went on again.

We came to the entrance of our house and got the door open. But then there were the stairs. You could manage by resting on your knees and taking a firm grip with both hands and waiting till you got your balance. Then you tightened your stomach and held your breath and pressed your wrists against your knees. Then quickly up and over the edge and you let your stomach go again and listened and waited, but the staircase was quite empty. And then the same thing all over again.

When the stairs narrowed and turned a corner, we had to move over to the wall side. We went on climbing slowly but no one came. Then I lay on top of the stone again and got my breath and looked at the silver, silver worth millions, and only four floors more and we would be there.

It happened when we got to the fourth floor. My hand slipped inside my mittens, I fell flat on my face and lay quite still and listened to the terrible noise of the stone falling. The noise got louder and louder, a noise like 'Crash, Crunch, Crack' all rolled into one, until the stone hit the Nieminens' door with a dull thud like doomsday.

It was the end of the world, and I covered my eyes with my mittens. Nothing happened. The echoes resounded up and down the stairs but nothing happened. No angry people opened their doors. Perhaps they were lying in wait inside.

I crept down on my hands and knees. Every step had a little semicircle bitten out of it. Further down they became big semicircles and the pieces lay everywhere and stared back at me. I rolled the stone away from the Nieminens' door and started all over again. We climbed up steadily and without looking at the chipped steps. We got past the place where things had gone wrong and took a rest in front of the balcony door. It's a dark-brown door and has tiny square panes of glass.

Then I heard the outside door downstairs open and shut, and somebody coming up the stairs. He climbed up and up with very slow steps. I crept forward to the banisters and looked down. I could see right to the bottom, a long narrow rectangle closed in by the banisters all the way down, and up the banisters came a great big hand, round and round and nearer and nearer. There was a mark in the middle of it, so I knew it was the tattooed hand of the caretaker, who was probably on his way up to the attic.

I opened the door to the balcony as quietly as I could and began to roll the stone over the threshold. The threshold was high. I rolled without thinking. I was very scared and couldn't get a good grasp and the stone rolled into the chink of the door and got wedged there. There were double doors with coiled iron springs at the top, which the caretaker had put there because women always forgot to shut the doors after them. I heard the springs contract and they sang softly to themselves as they squeezed me and the stone together between the doors and I put my legs together and took tight hold of the stone and tried to roll it but the space got narrower and narrower and I knew that the caretaker's hand was sliding up the banisters all the time.

I saw the silver of the stone quite close to my face and I gripped it and pushed and kicked with my legs and all of a sudden it tipped over and rolled several times and under the iron railing and into the air and disappeared.

Then I could see nothing but bits of fluff, light and airy as down, with small threads of colour here and there. I lay flat on my tummy and the door pinched my neck and everything was quiet until the stone reached the yard below. And there it exploded like a meteor; it covered the dustbins and the washing and all the steps and windows with silver! It made the whole of 4 Wharf Road look as if it was silver-plated and all the women ran to their windows thinking that war had broken out or doomsday had come! Every door opened and everybody ran up and down the stairs with the caretaker leading and saw how a wild animal had bitten bits out of every step and how a meteor had fallen out of a clear-blue sky.

But I lay squeezed in between the doors and said nothing. I didn't say anything afterwards, either. I never told anyone how close we had come to being rich.

Parties

SOMETIMES I WAS WOKEN UP IN THE MIDDLE OF THE night by the most beautiful music there is – balalaika and guitar. Daddy played the balalaika and Cavvy played the guitar. They played together very softly, almost in a whisper, both of them a long way away and then they sounded a little closer in turns so that sometimes it was the guitar that I heard and sometimes the balalaika.

They were gentle, sad songs about things that go on and on and that nobody can do anything about. Then they became wild and disorderly and Marcus broke his glass. But he never smashed more than one and Daddy made sure that he was always given one of the cheaper sort. Below the ceiling near my bed on the top bunk there was a cloud of grey tobacco smoke, and it made everything more unreal than it was. Perhaps we were out at sea or up in the mountains and I heard them shouting to each other through the cloud and things kept falling over and behind the violent noises came loud and soft waves of balalaika and guitar music.

I love Daddy's parties. They could go on for many nights of waking up and going to sleep again and being rocked by smoke and the music, and then suddenly a bellow would strike a chill right down to my toes.

It's not worth looking, because if you do everything you've imagined disappears. It's always the same. You can look down on them and there they are sitting on the sofa or on chairs or walking slowly up and down the room. Cavvy sits huddled up over his guitar as if he was hiding in it, his bald head floating around like a pale spot in the cloud, and he sinks lower and lower. Daddy sits very upright and looks straight ahead. The others doze off from time to time because having a party is very exhausting. But they won't go home because it's very important to make an effort to be the last. Daddy generally wins and is last. When all the others are asleep, he goes on staring and thinking till morning.

Mummy doesn't join in the party. She sees that the oil lamp doesn't start smoking in the bedroom. The bedroom is our only real room apart from the kitchen; I mean it has a door. But there is no stove in it. So the oil lamp must burn all night. If the door is opened the smoke gets into the bedroom and Per Olov gets asthma. Parties have been much more difficult since I got a brother but Mummy and Daddy try their best to arrange them all the same.

The table is the most beautiful thing. Sometimes I sit up and look over the railing and screw up my eyes and then the glasses and the candles and all the things on the table shimmer and make a whole as they do in a painting. Making a whole is very important. Some people just paint things and forget the whole, I know. I know a lot that I don't talk about.

All men have parties and are pals who never let each other down. A pal can say terrible things which are forgotten the next day. A pal never forgives, he just forgets, and a woman forgives but never forgets. That's how it is. That's why women aren't allowed to have parties. Being forgiven is very unpleasant.

A pal never says anything clever that's worth repeating the following day. He just feels that nothing is so important at the time.

Once Daddy and Cavvy played with a catapult that could shoot aeroplanes. I don't think Cavvy understood how it worked because he did it wrong and the aeroplane flew straight at his hand and the hook went right through it. It was awful and the blood ran all over the table and he couldn't even get his jacket on because the aeroplane wouldn't go through his sleeve. Daddy consoled him and took him to the hospital, where they snipped off the hook with pincers and put the aeroplane in the museum.

Anything can happen at a party if you aren't careful.

We never had a party in the studio, only in the living room. There are two high windows there which have a solemn-looking arch at the top and the whole of Grandmother's and Grandfather's curly-grained suite with scrolls all over it is there. It reminds Mummy of the house in the country where everything is just as it should be.

At first she was worried about the suite and was cross because of the cigarette burns and the marks left by glasses but by now she knows that it's all a question of patina.

Mummy is very good about parties. She never puts everything on the table and she never invites people. She knows that the only thing that really creates the right atmosphere is improvisation. Improvisation is a beautiful word. Daddy has to go out and look for his pals. They might be anywhere at any time. Sometimes he doesn't find anybody. But often he does. And then they feel like going somewhere. One always lands up somewhere. That's important.

Then someone says: "Let's look and see what we can find in the pantry." And one goes quietly to have a look and there's lots there! One finds expensive sausages and bottles and loaves of bread and butter and cheese and even soda water and then one carries everything in and improvises something. Mummy has everything ready.

Actually soda water is dangerous. It gives one bubbles in the tummy and it can make one feel very sad. One should never mix things.

Gradually all the candles on the balustrade go out and candle wax runs down onto the sofa. When the music is finished, there are war stories. Then I wait under the bedclothes but I always come up again when they attack the wicker chair. Then Daddy goes and fetches his bayonet, which hangs above the sacks of plaster in the studio, and everybody jumps up and shouts and Daddy attacks the chair. During the day it is covered with a rug so that you can't see what it looks like. After the wicker chair, Daddy doesn't want to play his balalaika any more. Then I just go to sleep.

The next day everybody is still there and they try to say nice things to me: "Good day pretty maiden," "How lovely 'twould be if you'd come a-walking this morning with me." Mummy gets presents. Ruokokoski once gave her half a pound of butter and another time she got a dozen eggs from Sallinen.

In the morning it's very important not to begin to tidy up too obviously. And if one lets in all that nasty fresh air, anyone can catch cold or get depressed. It's important to break the new day in very gradually and gently. Things look different in daylight, and if the difference seems too sudden everything can be spoilt. One must be able to move about in peace and quiet and see how one feels and wonder what it is one really wants to do.

One always wants something the next day, but one doesn't really know what. Finally one thinks that perhaps it's pickled herring. And so one goes into the pantry and has another look and there really is some pickled herring there.

And so the day goes on quietly and it's evening again and perhaps there are some new candles. Everyone behaves terribly cautiously because they know how little it takes to upset everything.

I go to bed and hear Daddy tuning his balalaika. Mummy lights the oil lamp. There's a completely round window in the bedroom. Nobody else has a round window. One can see out across all the roofs and over the harbour and gradually all the windows go dark except one. It is the one under Victor Ek's asbestos wall. There's a light on there all night. I think they're having a party there too. Or perhaps they're illustrating books.

The Dark

BEHIND THE RUSSIAN CHURCH THERE IS AN ABYSS. The moss and the rubbish are slippery and jagged old tins glitter at the bottom. For hundreds of years they have piled up higher and higher against a long dark red house without windows. The red house crawls round the rock and it is very significant that it has no windows. Behind the house is the harbour, a silent harbour with no boats in it. The little wooden door in the rock below the church is always locked.

"Hold your breath when you run past it," I told Poyu. "Otherwise Putrefaction will come out and catch you."

Poyu always has a cold. He can play the piano and holds his hands in front of him as if he were afraid of being attacked or was apologising to someone. I always scare him and he follows me because he wants to be scared.

As soon as twilight comes, a great big creature creeps over the harbour. It has no face but has got very distinct hands which cover one island after another as it creeps forward. When there are no more islands left, it stretches its arm out over the water, a very long arm that trembles a little and begins to grope its way towards Skatudden. Its fingers reach the Russian Church and touch the rock – oh! Such a great big grey hand!

I know what it is that's the worst thing of all. It's the skating-rink. I have a six-sided skating badge sewn to my jumper. The key I use to tighten my skates is on a shoelace round my neck. When you go down onto the ice, the skating-rink looks like a little bracelet of light far out in the darkness. The harbour is an ocean of blue snow and loneliness and nasty fresh air.

Poyu* doesn't skate because his ankles wobble, but I have to. Behind the rink lies the creeping creature and round the rink there is a ring of black water. The water breathes at the edge of the ice and moves gently, and sometimes it rises with a sigh and spreads out over the ice. When you are safely on the rink it isn't dangerous any more, but you feel gloomy.

Hundreds of shadowy figures skate round and round, all in the same direction, resolutely and pointlessly, and two freezing old men sit playing in the middle under a tarpaulin. They are playing "Ramona"and "I go out of an evening but my old girl stays at home". It is cold. Your nose runs, and when you wipe it you get icicles on

* Tove's friend Poyu would be known to Finnish readers as the renowned pianist and conductor Erik Tawaststjerna.

your mittens. Your skates have to be fixed to your heels. There's a little hole of iron and it's always full of small stones. I pick them out with the key of my skates. And then there are the stiff straps to thread through their holes. And then I go round with the others in order to get some fresh air and because the skating badge is very expensive. But there's no one here to scare, everybody just skates faster, strange shadows making scrunching and squeaking noises as they pass.

The lamps sway to and fro in the wind. If they went out we should keep going round and round in the dark, and the music would play on and on and gradually the channel in the ice would get wider and wider, yawning and breathing more heavily, and the whole harbour would be black water with only an island of ice on which we would go round and round for ever and ever amen.

Ramona is as pretty as a picture and as pale as The Thunder Bride. Ramona is for adults only. I have seen The Thunder Bride at the waxworks. Daddy and I love the waxworks. She was struck by lightning just when she was going to get married. The lightning struck her myrtle wreath and came out through her feet. That's why she is barefoot, and you can see quite clearly lots of crooked blue lines on the soles of her feet where the lightning came out again.

At the waxworks you can see how easy it is to smash people to pieces. They can be crushed, torn in half or sawn into little bits. Nobody is safe and therefore it is terribly important to find a hiding place in time.

I used to sing sad songs to Poyu. He put his hands over his ears but he listened all the same. Life is an isle of sorrow, you live today and die tomorrow! The skating -rink was the isle of sorrow. We drew it underneath the dining-room table. With a ruler Poyu drew every plank in the fence and the lamps all at the same distance from one another, and his pencil was always too hard. I only drew black and with a 4B – the darkness on the ice, or the channel in the ice or a thousand murky figures on squeaking skates flying round in a circle. He didn't understand what I was drawing, so I took a red pencil and whispered: "Marks of blood! Blood all over the ice!" And Poyu screamed while I captured this cruel thing on paper so that it couldn't get at me.

One Sunday I taught Poyu how to escape from the snakes in their big carpet. All you have to do is walk along the light-coloured edges, on all the colours that are light. If you step on the dark colours next to them, you are lost. There are such swarms of snakes there you just can't describe them, you have to imagine them. Everyone must imagine his own snakes because no one else's snakes can ever be as awful.

He balanced himself with tiny, tiny steps on the carpet, his hands in front of him and his great big wet handkerchief flapping in one hand.

"Now it's getting narrow," I said. "Look out for yourself and try to jump to that pale flower in the centre!"

The flower was almost right behind him and the pattern disappeared in a twirl. He tried desperately to keep his balance, flapped his handkerchief and began to scream, and then fell into the dark part. He screamed and screamed and rolled over on the carpet, rolled off onto the floor and under a cupboard. I screamed too, crawled after him and put my arms round him and held him tight until he calmed down.

People shouldn't have pile carpets – they're dangerous. It's much better to live in a studio with a concrete floor. That's why Poyu is always longing to come to our place.

We are busy digging a secret tunnel through the wall. I've got quite a long way and I only work when I'm alone. The wooden panelling went alright but then I had to use the marble hammer. Poyu's hole is much smaller, but his daddy's tools are so bad that it's a disgrace.

Every time I'm alone I take down the hanging on the wall and dig away, and no one has noticed what I am doing. The hanging is Mummy's. She painted it on sack-cloth when she was young. It shows an evening. There are straight tree-trunks rising out of the moss, and behind the tree-trunks the sky is red because the sun is setting. Everything except the sky has gone dark in a vague grey-ish brown but there are narrow red streaks that burn like fire. I love her picture. It goes deep into the wall, deeper than my hole, deeper than Poyu's drawing-room; it goes on endlessly and one never gets to the place where the sun is setting but the red gets more and more intense. I'm sure it's burning! There is a terrible fire, the kind of fire Daddy is always going out and waiting for.

The first time Daddy showed me his fire, it was winter. He went across the ice first and Mummy came behind him, pulling me on a sledge. It was the same red sky and the same shadowy figures running and something terrible had happened. There were jagged black things lying on the ice. Daddy collected them together and placed them in my lap. They were very heavy and pressed against my tummy.

'Explosion' is a beautiful word and a very big one. Later I learned others, the kind you can whisper only when you're alone. 'Inexorable'. 'Ornamentation'. 'Profile'. 'Catastrophic'. 'Electrical'. 'District nurse'.

They get bigger and bigger if you say them over and over again. You whisper and whisper and let the word grow until nothing exists except the word.

I wonder why fires always happen at night. Perhaps Daddy isn't interested in fires during the daytime because then the sky isn't red. He always woke us up and we heard the fire engine clanging; there was always a great rush and we ran through completely empty streets. It was always an awful long way to Daddy's fires. All the houses were asleep and the pointed chimneys were lifted upwards towards the red sky, which got nearer and nearer and at last we got there and Daddy lifted me up to see the fire. But sometimes it was a silly little fire that had already gone out long before we got there and then he was disappointed and had to be consoled.

Mummy only likes little fires like the ones she makes in ashtrays when no one is looking. And log-fires. She lights log-fires in the studio and in the passage every evening after Daddy has gone out looking for his friends.

When the log-fire is alight, we draw up the big chair. We turn out the lights in the studio and sit in front of the fire and she says: "Once upon a time there was a little girl who was terribly pretty and her mummy liked her so awfully much ..." Every story has to begin in the same way, then it's not so important what happens. A soft, gentle voice in the warm darkness and one gazes into the fire and nothing is dangerous. Everything else is outside and can't get in. Not now or at any time.

My mummy has lots of dark hair and it falls round you like a cloud, it smells nice and is like the hair of the sad queens in the book. The most beautiful picture covers a whole page. It shows a landscape at twilight, a plain covered with lilies. Pale queens are wandering over the whole plain with watering cans. The nearest one is indescribably beautiful. Her long dark hair is as soft as a cloud and the artist has covered it with sequins; probably some special finishing coat when the rest was done. Her profile is gentle and grave. And she walks there watering for the whole of her life and no one really knows how beautiful and how sad she is. The watering cans are painted with real silver, and how the publisher could afford such a thing neither Mummy nor I can understand.

Mummy's stories are often about Moses – in the bulrushes and later; about Isaac and about people who are homesick for their own country or get lost and then find their way again; about Eve and the Serpent in Paradise and great storms that die away in the end. Most of the people are homesick anyway, and a little lonely, and they hide themselves in their hair and are turned into flowers. Sometimes they are turned into frogs and

God keeps an eye on them the whole time and forgives them when he isn't angry and hurt and destroying whole cities because they believe in other gods.

Moses couldn't always control himself, either. But the women just waited and longed for their homes. Oh, I will lead you to your own country or to whatever country in the world you want and paint sequins in your hair and build a castle for you where we shall live until we die and never, never leave each other. Through endless forest dark and drear no comfort near a little girl alone did roam so far from home the way was long the night was cold the thunder rolled the girl did weep no more I'll find my mother kind for in this lonely haunted spot my awful lot will be beneath this tree to lie and slowly die.

Very satisfying. That's how it was when we shut the danger out.

Daddy's statues moved slowly round us in the light from the fire, his sad white ladies stepping warily, all ready to escape. They knew about the danger that lies in wait everywhere but nothing could save them until they were carved in marble and placed in a museum. There, one is safe. In a museum or in a lap or in a tree. Perhaps under the bedclothes. But the best thing of all is to sit high up in a tree; that is, if one isn't still inside one's mummy's tummy.

Snow

WHEN WE GOT TO THE STRANGE HOUSE IT BEGAN TO snow in quite a different way. A mass of tired old clouds opened and flung snow at us, all of a sudden and just anyhow. They weren't ordinary snowflakes – they fell straight down in large sticky lumps, they clung to each other and sank quickly and they weren't white, but grey. The whole world was as heavy as lead.

Mummy carried in the suitcases and stamped her feet on the doormat and talked the whole time because she thought the whole thing was such fun and that everything was different.

But I said nothing because I didn't like this strange house. I stood in the window and watched the snow falling, and it was all wrong. It wasn't the same as in town. There it blows black and white over the roof or falls gently as if from heaven, and forms beautiful arches over the sitting-room window. The landscape looked dangerous too. It was bare and open and swallowed up the snow, and the trees stood in black rows that ended in nothing. At the edge of the world there was a narrow fringe of forest. Everything was wrong. It should be winter in town and summer in the country. Everything was topsy-turvy.

The house was big and empty, and there were too many rooms. Everything was very clean and you could never hear your own steps as you walked because the carpets were so big and they were as soft as fur.

If you stood in the furthest room, you could see through all the other rooms and it made you feel sad; it was like a train ready to leave with its lights shining over the platform. The last room was dark like the inside of a tunnel except for a faint glow in the gold frames and the mirror which was hung too high on the wall. All the lamps were soft and misty and made a very tiny circle of light. And when you ran you made no noise.

It was just the same outside. Soft and vague, and the snow went on falling and falling.

I asked why we were living in this strange house but got no proper answer. The person who cooked the food was hardly ever to be seen and didn't talk. She padded in without one noticing her and then out again. The door swung to without a sound and rocked backwards and forwards for a long time before it was still. I showed that I didn't like this house by keeping quiet. I didn't say a word.

In the afternoon the snow was even greyer and fell in flocks and stuck to the window-panes and then slid down and new flocks appeared out of the twilight and replaced them. They were like grey hands with a hundred fingers. I tried to watch one all the way as it fell, it spread out and fell, faster and faster. I stared at the next one and the next one and in the end my eyes began to hurt and I got scared.

It was hot everywhere and there was enough room for crowds of people but there were only two of us. I said nothing.

Mummy was happy and rushed all over the place saying: "What peace and quiet! Isn't it lovely and warm!" And so she sat down at a big shiny table and began to draw. She took the lace tablecloth off and spread out all her illustrations and opened the bottle of Indian ink.

Then I went upstairs. The stairs creaked and groaned and made lots of noises that stairs make when a family has gone up and down them for ages. That's good. Stairs should do that sort of thing. One knows exactly which step squeaks and which one doesn't and where one has to tread if one doesn't want to make oneself heard. It was just that this staircase wasn't our staircase. Quite a different family had used it. Therefore I thought this staircase was creepy.

Upstairs all the soft lamps were on in the same way and all the rooms were warm and tidy and all the doors were standing open. Only one door was closed. Inside, it was cold and dark. It was the box room. The other family's belongings were lying there in packing-cases and

trunks and there were mothproof bags hanging in long rows with a little snow on top of them.

Now I could hear the snow. It was falling all the time, whispering and rustling to itself and in one corner it had crept onto the floor.

The other family was everywhere in there, so I shut the door and went down again and said I wanted to go to bed. Actually I didn't want to go to bed at all, but I thought it would be best. Then I wouldn't have to say anything. The bed was as wide and desolate as the landscape. outside. The eiderdown was like a hand, too. You sank and sank right to the bottom of the earth under a big soft hand. Nothing was like it was at home, or like anywhere else.

In the morning it was still snowing in just the same way. Mummy had already got started with her work and was very cheerful. She didn't have to light fires or get meals ready and didn't have to be worried about anybody. I said nothing.

I went to the furthest room and watched the snow. I had a great responsibility and had to see what the snow was doing. It had risen since yesterday. A thousand tons of wet snow had slithered down the window-panes, and I had to climb onto a chair to see the long grey landscape. The snow had risen out there, too. The trees were thinner and more timid and the horizon had moved further away. I looked at everything until I knew that soon we would be done for. This snow had decided to go on falling until everything was a single, vast wet snowdrift, and nobody would remember what had been underneath it.

All the trees would sink into the earth and all the houses. No roads and no tracks – just snow falling and falling and falling.

I went up to the boxroom and listened to it falling, I heard how it stuck fast and grew. I couldn't think of anything but the snow.

Mummy went on drawing.

I was building with the cushions on the sofa and sometimes I looked at her through a peephole between them. She felt me looking and asked: "Are you alright?" While she went on drawing. And I answered: "Of course". Then I crept on hands and knees into the end room and climbed onto a chair and saw how the snow was sinking down over me. Now the whole horizon had crept below the edge of the world. The fringe of forest couldn't be seen any longer; it had slid over. The world had capsized, it was turning over quietly, a little bit every day.

The very thought of it made me feel giddy. Slowly, slowly, the world was turning, heavy with snow. The trees and houses were no longer upright. They were slanting. Soon it would be difficult to walk straight. All the people on earth would have to creep. If they had forgotten to fasten their windows, they would burst open. The doors would burst open. The water barrels would fall over and begin to roll over the endless field and out over the edge of the world. The whole world was full of things rolling, slithering and falling. Big things rumbled, you could hear them from far off, and you had to work out where they would come, and get away from them. Here they were, rumbling past, leaping in the snow when the angle was too great, and finally falling into space. Small houses without cellars broke loose and whirled away. The snow stopped falling downwards, it flew horizontally. It fell upwards and disappeared. Everything that couldn't hold on tight rolled out into space, and slowly the sky went dark and turned black. We crept under the furniture between the windows, taking care not to tread on the glass. But from time to time a picture or a lamp bracket fell and smashed the window-pane. The house groaned and the plaster came loose. And outside, large heavy objects rumbled past, rolling right through the whole of Finland all the way down from the Arctic Circle, and they were even heavier because they had collected so much snow as they rolled and sometimes people fell past screaming all the time.

The snow on the ground began to slither away. It slid in an enormous avalanche which grew and grew over the edge of the world ... oh no! oh no!

I rolled backwards and forwards on the carpet to make the horror of it seem greater, and in the end I saw the wall heave over me and the pictures hung straight out on their wires.

"What are you doing?" Mummy asked.

Then I lay still and said nothing.

"Shall we have a story?" she asked, and went on drawing.

But I didn't want any other story than this one of my own. But one doesn't say that sort of thing. So I said: "Come up and look at the attic."

Mummy dried her Indian ink pen and came with me. We stood in the attic and froze for a while and Mummy said "It's lonely here," so we went back into the warmth again and she forgot to tell me a story. Then I went to bed.

Next morning the daylight was green, underwater lighting throughout the room. Mummy was asleep. I got up and opened the door and saw that the lamps were on in all the rooms although it was morning and the green light came through the snow which covered the windows all the way up. Now it had happened. The house was a single enormous snowdrift, and the surface of the ground was somewhere high up above the roof. Soon the trees would creep down into the snow until only their tops stuck out, and then the tops would disappear too and everything would level itself off and be flat. I could see it, I knew. Not even praying would stop it.

I became very solemn and quite calm and sat down on the carpet in front of the blazing fire.

Mummy woke up and came in and said, "Look how funny it is with snow covering the windows," because she didn't understand how serious it all was. When I told her what had really happened, she became very thoughtful.

"In fact," she said after a while, "we have gone into hibernation. Nobody can get in any longer and no one can get out!"

I looked carefully at her and understood that we were saved. At last we were absolutely safe and protected. This menacing snow had hidden us inside in the warmth for ever and we didn't have to worry a bit about what went on there outside. I was filled with enormous relief, and I shouted, "I love you, I LOVE YOU," and took all the cushions and threw them at her and laughed and shouted and Mummy threw them all back, and in the end we were lying on the floor just laughing.

Then we began our underground life. We walked around in our nighties and did nothing. Mummy didn't draw. We were bears with pine needles in our stomachs and anyone who dared come near our winter lair was torn to pieces. We were lavish with the wood, and threw log after log onto the fire until it roared.

Sometimes we growled. We let the dangerous world outside look after itself; it had died, it had fallen out into space. Only Mummy and I were left.

It began in the room at the end. At first it was the nasty scraping sound made by shovels. Then the snow fell down over the windows and grey light came in everywhere. Somebody tramped past outside and came to the next window and let in more light. It was awful.

The scraping sound went along the whole row of windows until the lamps were burning as if at a funeral. Outside snow was falling. The trees were standing in rows and were as black as they had been before and they let the snow fall on them and the fringe of forest on the horizon was still there.

We went and got dressed. Mummy sat down to draw.

A dark man went on shovelling outside the door and all of a sudden I started to cry and I screamed: "I'll bite him! I'll go outside and bite him!"

"I shouldn't do that," Mummy said. "He wouldn't understand." She screwed the top onto the bottle of Indian ink and said: "What about going home?"

"Yes," I said.

So we went home.

German Measles

I HAD GERMAN MEASLES; I LAY IN BED IN MY BUNK trying to crochet a kettle-holder. The eiderdown was a mountain landscape with small plaster animals wandering up and down and never getting anywhere. In the end I made an earthquake and they lay flat and didn't have to make an effort any more.

Poppolino sat in his cage on Daddy's bunk rummaging in his bits of newspaper. He lifted them up one by one and then threw them down again as if they disgusted him, stared at the ceiling and scratched his backside. His eyes looked very yellow in the wintry light.

Suddenly he was scared by his own tail, which was sticking out from under the newspapers as though it was a snake. He screamed and rushed up his tree and flung himself against the bars and shook the cage so that masses of plaster fell off the ceiling. Then he sat still looking like a miserable rat all hunched up. He pulled his long upper lip down and stared straight ahead and let his hands flop as if nothing was worth the effort. Then he fell asleep.

It was a tedious day. I turned towards the cardboard dividing wall and looked down into the studio through my secret peephole.

Mummy was at the Mint drawing. Daddy stood in front of the modelling stand with his clay rags in his hands. He flung them onto the box of clay and swung the revolving chassis round so that it squeaked. Then he stepped backwards and looked.

He swung the chassis again and stood looking for a long while. Then he went over to the window and looked down into the street. He moved a tin and went into the sitting-room and looked out of that window. Then he went and fetched some water to water the ivy.

I turned over and tried to go to sleep but couldn't. After a while the modelling stand squeaked again. Then I heard that Daddy had gone back into the sitting-room and was rattling the loose change and nails that he had in the pockets of his overalls. He turned on the wireless and put on the headphones. Then he turned it off again and took the headphones off.

Poppolino woke up and began to scream. He shook the cage and put his face between the bars and screamed as he looked at Daddy in the sitting-room. Daddy climbed up onto his bunk and sat in front of the cage and talked very softly and I couldn't hear what he said.

He opened the door and tried to put Poppolino's collar on. But Poppolino slunk away and jumped onto the sitting-room sofa and went into the studio. Then all was quiet.

Daddy climbed down again and called Poppolino. He called in his kind and treacly voice that made me very cross. Now they were both in the studio.

Poppolino was sitting on a plaster bust close to the ceiling, gaping. Daddy stood below calling him enticingly. Then it happened again.

Poppolino started swinging on the bust and then sprang. It was a big bust of an alderman and there was a frightful noise as it smashed to smithereens all over the floor. Poppolino clung to the curtains and shrieked with fright and Daddy said nothing. Then something just as big crashed to the floor, but I only heard the noise as I daren't look any longer.

When all was quiet again I assumed that Poppolino had taken refuge on Daddy's shoulder and was being consoled. In a while they would go out for a walk in the park. I listened carefully. Then Daddy put on Poppolino's velvet jacket and hat. Daddy talked the whole time he was doing up the buttons and the hat ribbon, and Poppolino was saying how rotten and beastly everything was. Now they were out in the hall. The door made a clicking noise as they went out.

I got out of bed and took all my plaster animals and threw them down into the sitting- room. I climbed down the steps and fetched the hammer and bashed them to powder and rubbed the plaster into the carpet with

my feet. Then I climbed up and crept into Poppolino's cage. I sat in his bits of newspaper and breathed German measles on everything as hard as I could.

When they came home again I could tell that they had been to the shop and bought liquorice and herrings. I lay under the bedclothes and heard Daddy put Poppolino back into his cage. He talked away in a cheerful voice and I took it that Poppolino had been given some liquorice. Then Daddy came over to my bunk and tried to give me some liquorice too.

"Monkey food!" I said. "I don't want to eat the same things as someone who smashes statues."

"But it wasn't a good one," Daddy said. "It was good that Poppolino knocked it over. How do you feel now?"

"I shall soon be dead," I answered, and crept lower down the bed.

"Don't be silly," Daddy said. When I didn't answer he went into the studio and started working. He was whistling. I heard him walking up and down in front of the modelling stand, whistling and working.

I felt my guilty conscience in my toes, and before it could creep any higher I sat up quickly and started to crochet. I wasn't going to make a kettle-holder any longer. It would be a pullover for Poppolino.

It's difficult to tell why or how people cheer up and get the feeling they want to work. It's not easy to be sure about germs, either. Best not to think about it too much but try and put everything right as quickly as possible with a good deed.

Flying

I DREAMED THAT THOUSANDS OF PEOPLE WERE RUNNING in the street. They weren't shouting but you could hear the sound of their boots on the pavement, many thousands of boots, and there was a red glow in the studio from outside. After a while there weren't so many of them running, and in the end there were only the steps of the last one, who was running in such a way that he fell over and then picked himself up and ran on.

Then everything started shrinking. Every piece of furniture became elongated and narrow and disappeared towards the ceiling. There was something crawling under the rag rugs in the hall. It was also narrow and thin and wriggled in the middle, sometimes very quickly and sometimes very slowly.

I tried to get into the bedroom where Mummy had lit the oil lamp but the door was shut. Then I ran up the steps to the bunk. The door of Poppolino's cage was open and I could hear him padding round somewhere in the dark and whining, which is something he always does when it is very cold or when he feels lonely.

Now it came up the steps, grey and limping. One of its legs had come off. It was the ghost of the dead crow. I flew into the sitting-room and bumped about on the ceiling like a fly. I could see the sitting-room and the studio underneath me in a deep well that sank deeper and deeper.

I thought more about that dream afterwards, particularly about the flying part, and decided to fly as often as possible.

But it didn't work and I dreamed about all the wrong things, and in the end I made up my own dreams myself just before I went to sleep or just after I had woken up. I started by thinking up the most awful things I could, which wasn't particularly difficult. When I had made things as awful as possible I took a run and bounced off the floor and flew away from everything, leaving it all behind me in a deep well. Down there the whole town was burning. Down there Poppolino was padding around in the studio in the dark screaming with loneliness. Down there sat the crow saying: "It was your fault that I died." And the Unmentionable Thing crawled under the mat.

But I just went on flying. In the beginning I bumped about on the ceiling like a fly, but then I ventured out of the window. Straight across the street was the farthest I could fly. But if I glided I could go on as long as I wanted, right down to the bottom of the well. There I took another leap and flew up again.

It wasn't long before they caught sight of me. At first they just stopped and stared, then they started to shout and point and came running from all directions. But before they could reach me I had taken another leap and was up in the air again laughing and waving at them. They tried to jump after me. They ran to fetch step-ladders and fishing-rods but nothing helped. There they were, left behind below me, longing to be able to fly. Then they went slowly home and got on with their work.

Sometimes they had too much work to do and sometimes they just couldn't work, which was horrid for them. I felt sorry for them and made it possible for them all to fly.

Next morning they all woke up with no idea of what had happened and sat up and said: "Another miserable day begins!" They climbed down from their bunks and drank some warm milk and had to eat the skin too. Then they put on their coats and hats and went downstairs and off to their work, dragging their legs and wondering whether they should take the tram.

But then they decided to walk in any case, because one is allowed to take a tram for seven stops but not really for five, and in any case fresh air is healthy.

One of them came down Wharf Road and a lot of wet snow stuck to her boots. So she stamped a little to

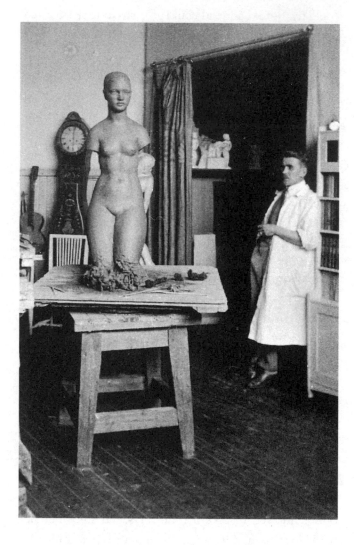

get rid of the snow – and, sure enough, she flew into the air! Only about six feet, and then came down again and stood wondering what had happened to her. Then she noticed a gentleman running to catch the tram. It rang its bell and was off so he ran even faster and the next moment he was flying too. He took off from the ground and described an arc in the air up to the roof of the tram and there he sat!

Then Mummy began to laugh as hard as she could and immediately understood what had happened and cried "Ha! ha! ha!" and flew onto Victor Ek's roof in a single beautiful curve. There she caught sight of Daddy in the studio window rattling nails and coins in the pockets of his overall and she shouted: "Jump out! Come flying with me!"

But Daddy daren't until Mummy flew over and sat on the windowsill. Then he opened the window and took hold of her hand and flew out and said: "Well, I'll be damned!"

By that time the whole of Helsinki was full of amazed people flying. No one did any work. Windows were open all over the place and down in the street the trams and the cars were empty and it stopped snowing and the sun came out.

All the new-born babies were flying and all the very old people and their cats and dogs and guinea-pigs and monkeys – just everybody!

Even the President was out flying!

The roofs were crowded with picnickers undoing their sandwiches and opening bottles and shouting: "Cheers!"

to one another across the street and everyone was doing precisely what he or she wanted to do.

I stood in the bedroom window watching the whole thing and enjoying myself no end and wondering how long I should let them go on flying. And I thought that if I now made everything normal again it might be dangerous. Imagine what would happen if the following morning they all opened their windows and jumped out! Therefore I decided that they could be allowed to go on flying until the end of the world in Helsinki.

Then I opened my bedroom window and climbed onto the window-ledge together with the crow and Poppolino. "Don't be afraid!" I said. And so off we flew.

Annie

IT WAS SO NICE LOOKING AT ANNIE. ANNIE'S HAIR GREW like luscious rough grass; it looked as if it had been cut any old how and was so full of life that it crackled. Her eyebrows were just as thick and black and met in the middle, her nose was flat and she had very pink cheeks. Her arms plunged into the washing-up water like pillars. She was beautiful.

Annie sings while she's washing up and I sit under the table and try to learn the words. I've got to the thirteenth verse of Lord Henry and Fair Hilda and that's where things actually start to happen.

The sound of a charger was heard in the hall and harpist and fiddler and wedding guests all were filled with such horror, for yea it is told Lord Henry rode in clad as warrior bold. Lo! Vengeance be mine and in blood for this day oh Hilda so fair you our love do betray pale ghost of a bride on your penitent knee the wrath of my upraised arm you shall see. It makes you shiver it's so beautiful. It's the same for Annie when she says: "You must go out for a while because I want to cry, it's so beautiful."

Annie's lovers often come clad as warriors bold. I liked the dragoon in red trousers with gold braid on his jacket; he was so handsome. He took off his sword. Sometimes it fell on the floor and I could hear it rattle from all the way up on my bunk – and thought of the wrath of his upraised arm. Then he disappeared and Annie got another lover who was a Thinking Man. So she went to listen to Plato and despised Daddy because he read newspapers and Mummy because she read novels.

I explained to Annie that Mummy had no time to read any books other than those she had to draw the jackets for so that she could find out what the book was about and what the heroine looked like. Some people just draw as they like and don't give a fig for the author. That's wrong. An illustrator has to think of the author and the reader and sometimes even of the publisher.

"Huh!" said Annie. "It's a rubbishy old firm that doesn't publish Plato. Anyway, everything the mistress draws for she gets free and on the last jacket the heroine didn't have yellow hair although it was yellow in the book."

"Colour is expensive!" I said and got angry. "Anyhow, she has to pay fifty per cent for some of the books!"

It was impossible to explain to Annie that publishers don't like to print in many colours and that they go on about two-colour printing although they know that one of the colours must be black anyway and that one can draw hair without using yellow and make it look yellow all the same.

"Is that so?" said Annie. "And what has that to do with Plato, if I might ask?"

Then I forgot what it was I had to say. Annie always got things mixed up and was always right in the end.

But sometimes I bullied her. I made her tell me about her childhood until she started to cry and then I just stood in the window, rocking backwards and forwards on my heels and staring down at the yard. Or I stopped asking questions although her face was swollen and she threw the dustpan right across the kitchen. I could bully Annie by being polite to her lovers and asking them questions about things that interested them and just not going away and leaving them alone. And a very good way was to put on a haughty drawling voice and say, "The mistress wants roast veal on Sunday," and then leave immediately as if Annie and I had nothing else to say to each other.

Annie got her revenge with Plato for a long time. Once she had a lover who was a Man of the People, and then she got her revenge by talking about all the old women who got up at four o'clock in the morning to deliver newspapers while the master lay lounging in bed waiting for the morning paper. I said that no old woman in the world who delivered newspapers worked all night making a plaster cast for a competition, and that Mummy worked till two o'clock every night while Annie lay in bed lounging, and then Annie said, "Don't mix me up in all this, and anyway the master didn't get a prize last time!" Then I shouted that it was because the jury had been unfair and she shouted that it was easy to say that and I said that she didn't understand a thing about it because she wasn't an artist and she said that it was all very well to get all superior when some people hadn't even been taught to draw, and so we didn't speak to each other for several hours.

When we had both had a good cry, I went into the kitchen again and Annie had hung a blanket over the kitchen table. This meant that I was allowed to play houses under the table provided that I didn't get in her way or block the pantry door. I built my house with logs and chairs and stools. I only did it out of politeness because actually you could build a much better house under the big modelling stand in the studio.

When the house was ready, she gave me some crockery. I took this out of politeness, too. I don't like pretending to cook. I hate food.

Once there was no bird-cherry in the market for the first of June. Mummy has to have bird-cherry for her birthday; otherwise she will die. That's what a gypsy told her when she was fifteen years old and since then everyone has always made a terrible fuss about bird-cherry. Sometimes it comes out too early and sometimes too late. If you bring it into the house in the middle of May, it goes brown round the edges and the flowers never really come out.

But Annie said: "I know there is a white bird-cherry in the park. We'll go and pick some when it gets dark."

It was terribly late when it got dark, but I was allowed to go with her in any case and we didn't say a word about what we were going to do. Annie took my hand – her hands are always damp and warm – and as she moved there was a smell about her that was hot and a little frightening. We went down Wharf Road and across to the park and I was scared stiff and thought about the park keeper and the Town Council and God.

"Daddy would never do anything like this," I said.

"No, he wouldn't," Annie said. "The master's far too bourgeois. You just help yourself to what you want, and that's all there is to it."

We had climbed over the fence before I had really grasped the unthinkable thing she had said about Daddy being bourgeois. I was so taken aback that I didn't have time to be offended.

Annie strode up to the white bush in the middle of the grass and began picking. "You're doing it wrong!" I hissed. "Do it properly."

Annie stood upright in the grass with her legs apart and looked at me. She opened her big mouth and laughed so that you could see all her beautiful white teeth and she took me by the hand again and crouched down and we ran under the bushes and began to creep away. We sneaked up to another white bush and Annie was looking over her shoulder the whole time and sometimes she stopped behind a tree. "Is it better this way?" she asked.

I nodded and squeezed her hand. Then she started picking again. She reached up with her enormous arms so that her dress stretched tight all over and she laughed and broke off the boughs and the flowers rained all over her face and I whispered "Stop, stop, that's enough," and I was so beside myself with fright and ecstasy that I almost wet my knickers.

"If you're going to steal you might as well steal properly," Annie said calmly. Her arms were full of bird-cherry, it lay across her neck and shoulders and she clasped it firmly with her red hands. We climbed back over the fence and went home and there was no sign of a park keeper or a policeman.

Then they told us that the bush we had picked from wasn't a bird-cherry at all. It was just white. But Mummy was alright, she didn't die.

Sometimes Annie would get mad and shout: "I can't stand the sight of you! Get out!" Then I would go down into the yard and sit on the rubbish bin and burn old rolls of film with a magnifying glass.

I love smells. The smell of burning films, the smell of heat and Annie and the box of clay in the studio and Mummy's hair and the smell of parties and bird-cherry. I haven't got a smell yet; at least I don't think so.

Annie smelt differently in the summer – of grass – and even warmer. She laughed more often and you could see more of her arms and legs.

Annie could really row. She took a single pull and then rested on the oars in triumph and the boat glided forward over the sound so that there was a splashing round the bows in the still water of evening and then she took another pull and the boat splashed again and Annie showed how strong she was. Then she would laugh loudly and put one oar in the water so that the boat swung round to show that she didn't want to go in any particular direction but was just amusing herself. In the end she just let the boat drift, and lay in the bottom and sang, and everybody on the shore heard her singing in the sunset and they knew that there she lay, big and happy and warm and not caring a fig for anything. She was doing just what she wanted to do.

Then she would stroll up the slope, her whole body swaying to and fro, and now and then she would pause to pick a flower. Annie used to sing when she was baking, too. She kneaded the dough, rolled it out, patted it, shaped it and threw her buns into the oven so that they landed exactly in the right place on the tray and then she slammed the oven door and cried, "Oh! It's so hot!"

I love Annie in the summertime and I never bully her then.

Sometimes we went to Diamond Valley. It's a beach where all the pebbles are round and precious and beautiful colours. They're prettier under the water, but if you rub them with margarine they're always pretty. We went there once when Mummy and Daddy were working in town, and when we had gathered enough diamonds we sat and rested on the hill slope. In the early summer and autumn there are always streams coming down the slope. We made waterfalls and dams.

"There's gold in the stream," Annie said. "See if you can find it." I couldn't see any gold.

"You have to put it there yourself," said Annie. "Gold looks wonderful in brown water. It multiplies. More and more gold." So I went home and fetched all the gold things we possessed and the pearls as well, and put them all in the stream and they looked terribly beautiful.

Annie and I lay in the grass and listened to the sound of the stream and she sang 'Full Fathom Five'. She stepped into the water and picked up Mummy's gold bracelet with her toes and dropped it again and laughed. Then she said: "I've always longed to have things of real gold."

Next day all the gold had disappeared and the pearls too. I thought it was odd. "You never know what streams will do," Annie said. "Sometimes the gold grows and grows and sometimes it vanishes under the ground. But it can come up again if you don't talk about it." So we went home and made some pancakes.

In the evening Annie went to meet her new lover at the village swing. He was a Man of Action and could make the swing go right round, and the only person who dared to sit on it while it went round four times was Annie.

PART II

Flotsam and Jetsam

The Iceberg

THE SUMMER CAME SO EARLY THAT YEAR THAT IT MIGHT almost have been called spring – it was a kind of present and everything one did had to be thought out differently. It was cloudy and very calm.

We and our luggage were the same as usual, and so were Old Charlie and Old Charlie's boat, but the beaches were bare and forbidding and the sea looked stern. And when we had rowed as far as Newness Island the iceberg came floating towards us.

It was green and white and sparkling and it was coming in order to meet me. I had never seen an iceberg before.

Now it all depended on whether anyone said anything. If they said a single word about the iceberg, it wouldn't be mine any longer.

We got closer and closer. Daddy rested on his oars but Old Charlie went on rowing and said: "It's early this year." And Daddy answered, "Yes. It's not long since it broke up," and went on rowing.

Mummy didn't say a thing.

Anyway, you couldn't count that as actually saying anything about an iceberg, and so this iceberg was mine.

We rowed past it but I didn't turn round to look because then they might have said something. I just thought about it all the way along Batch Island. My iceberg looked like a tattered crown. On one side there was an oval-shaped grotto which was very green and closed in by a grating of ice. Under the water the ice was a different green, which went very deep down and was almost black where the dangerous depths began. I knew that the iceberg would follow me and I wasn't the least bit worried about it.

I sat in the bay all day long and waited. Evening came but still the iceberg hadn't reached me. I said nothing, and no one asked me anything. They were all busy unpacking.

When I went to bed the wind had got up. I lay under the bedclothes and imagined I was an ice mermaid listening to the wind rising. It was important not to fall asleep but I did anyway, and when I woke up the house was completely quiet. Then I got up and dressed and took Daddy's torch and went out onto the steps.

It was a light night, but it was the first time I had been out alone at night and I thought about the iceberg all the time so that I wouldn't get frightened. I didn't light the torch. The landscape was just as forbidding as before and looked like an illustration in which, for once, they had printed the grey shades properly. Out at sea the long-tailed ducks were carrying on like mad, singing wedding songs to one another.

Even before I got to the field by the shore I could see the iceberg. It was waiting for me and was shining just as beautifully but very faintly. It was lying there bumping against the rocks at the end of the point where it was deep, and there was deep black water and just the wrong distance between us. If it had been shorter I should have jumped over; if it had been a little longer I could have thought: 'What a pity, no one can manage to get over that.'

Now I had to make up my mind. And that's an awful thing to have to do.

The oval grotto with the grating of ice was facing the shore and the grotto was as big as me. It was made for a little girl who pulled up her legs and cuddled them to her. There was room for the torch too.

I lay down flat on the rock, reached out with my hand and broke off one of the icicles in the grating. It was so cold, it felt hot. I held onto the grating with both hands and could feel it melting. The iceberg was moving as one does when one breathes – it was trying to come to me.

My hands and my tummy began to feel icy-cold and I sat up. The grotto was the same size as me, but I didn't dare to jump. And if one doesn't dare to do something immediately, then one never does it.

I switched on the torch and threw it into the grotto. It fell on its side and lit up the whole grotto, making it just as beautiful as I had imagined it would be. It became an illuminated aquarium at night, the manger at Bethlehem or the biggest emerald in the world! It was so unbearably beautiful that I had to get away from the whole thing as quickly as possible, send it away, do something! So I sat down firmly and placed both feet on the iceberg and pushed it as hard as I could. It didn't move.

"Go away!" I shouted. "Clear off!"

And then the iceberg glided very slowly away from me and was caught by the offshore wind. I was so cold that I ached and saw the iceberg carried by the wind towards the sound – it would sail right out to sea with Daddy's torch on board and the ducks would sing themselves hoarse when they saw an illuminated bridal barge coming towards them.

And so my honour was saved.

When I got to the steps, I turned round and looked. My iceberg shone steadily out there like a green beacon and the batteries would last until sunrise because they were always new when one had just moved to the country. Perhaps they would last another night; perhaps the torch would go on shining at the bottom of the sea after the iceberg had melted and turned into water.

I got into bed and pulled the bedclothes over my head and waited for the warmth to come back. It came. Slowly at first, but little by little it reached down to my feet.

But all the same I had been a coward, and all because of two inches. I could feel it in my tummy. Sometimes I think all strong feelings start in the tummy; for me they do, at any rate.

Albert

ALBERT IS ONE YEAR OLDER THAN I AM, IF YOU DON'T count six days.

For six days we are the same age.

He sat in the bay where the boats were and baited his father's long-line with bleak fish.

"You must kill them first," I said. "It's awful putting a hook in them while they're still alive."

Albert raised a shoulder slightly and I knew that it meant some kind of excuse and explanation: "Fish bite better if the bait is alive." He was wearing very faded overalls and a black cap that made his ears stick out.

"How would you like to have a hook put through your back?" I said. "You'd be caught and you'd scream and try to get free and you'd just wait to be eaten up! What?"

"They don't scream," said Albert. "It's always done like this."

"You're cruel!" I shouted. "You do awful things. I don't want to talk to you any more!"

He looked up at me a little sadly under his peaked cap and said: "There, there!" Then he went on putting the bleak on the line.

I walked away. At the boathouse I turned round and shouted: "I'm just as old as you are! I'M JUST AS OLD AS YOU ARE!"

"Yes, I suppose you are," Albert replied.

I went and knocked nails into the raft but it wasn't any fun. Three nails went in crooked and I couldn't get them out again.

I went down to the beach again and said: "Fish suffer just as much as people do."

"I don't think they do," said Albert. "They're a lower form of life."

I said: "How can you tell? Imagine if trees suffer as well! You saw them in half and they scream although you can't hear anything. Flowers scream when you pick them, though only a little bit."

"Perhaps they do," said Albert. He said it in a very kind way but, even so, a little patronisingly and that made me angry again.

It was a nasty day. It was hazy and hot and sticky. I tried to cheer myself up by going to sit on the roof and sat there for a long time. I saw Albert and Old Charlie row out with the long-line. On the horizon there was a dirty-looking bank of clouds stretching all the

way from Acre Island to Black Ball and the sea was completely smooth.

Then they came back and pulled up the boat.

After a while I could hear Albert knocking nails into the raft. I climbed down the ladder and went over to him and watched.

"You knock nails in well," I said.

Then he hammered even more violently so that every nail went in with five blows. I began to feel better. I sat down in the grass and watched him and counted the hammer blows out loud. One nail went in with four. Then we both laughed.

"Let's take it out straight away," I said. "Now. We'll find a roller and get it into the sea at once."

We dragged up two planks and put a pit-prop across them and lifted the raft onto it. It was heavy and it creaked and bent a bit, but we got it up. Then all we had to do was roll it. The raft entered the water and glided out into the bay. It sat in the water beautifully. Albert went to fetch the paddles and we waded out, gave the raft a shove and jumped on. A little water came over the top but not much. We looked at each other and laughed.

It was slow work paddling, but we got going. We reached deep water, but that was alright because we had both nearly learned to swim. After a while we entered the sound near Red Rock.

"Let's go to Sandy Island," I said.

"I'm not so sure about that," Albert answered. "It's going to get foggy."

But I paddled on and we moved slowly towards Sandy Island. We punted ourselves along the shore and past the point. The sea was just as smooth and the bank of dirty clouds had grown and reached Egg Island. Albert pointed and said, "That's fog. Now we're going home."

"You aren't afraid of a little fog, are you?" I asked. "Let's go a little bit further and then we'll turn round."

"I'm not so sure about that," said Albert.

"You're not scared, are you?" I said, and he paddled on and the raft went out to sea again. It was like moving across a black mirror, like standing on the sea; one could feel the faint swell all through one's body and one moved with it. The swell came from the south-east and rolled on towards Egg Island.

"We're turning round now," said Albert firmly. "The fog's coming."

It got cold very quickly and the fog was there, moving thickly around us, shutting us in on all sides. The smooth swell rolled out of the fog, crawled under the raft with a swallowing movement and rolled back into the fog the other side. I was freezing and was waiting for Albert to say, "What did I say?" or "I told you so ...", but he was silent and just paddled on and looked worried. He turned his head this way and that and listened and looked at the swell and kept in to the shore. After a while he kept more out to sea instead. Now there was a cross-wave in the swell and it started to come from all directions at the same time. Albert stopped paddling and said: "We'd better wait until it lifts."

I was a little scared and said nothing at all.

"If only Rosa would moo, we'd get our direction," said Albert.

We listened in the fog but Rosa didn't moo. Everything was as silent and deserted as the place where the world ends, and terribly cold.

"Look, there's something floating," said Albert.

It was greyish-white and straggly and was moving very slowly in a circle towards us in the swell.

Albert said: "It's a herring gull." He poked it with the paddle and lifted it up onto the raft. It looked very big on the raft and went on shuffling round in a circle.

"It's not well," I said. "It's in pain."

Albert picked it up by the neck and looked at it, and it began to screech and flap one wing.

"Let it go!" I shouted. Everything looked so terrifying with the fog and the black water and the bird creeping around and screaming that I was beside myself and said: "Give it to me, I'll hold it in my lap. We must make it well again."

I sat down on the raft and Albert laid the bird in my lap and said: "It won't get well. We must kill it."

"You're always killing and killing," I said. "Look how it's cuddling up to me; it's lonely and unhappy!"

But Albert said, "It's got worms," and lifted up one wing and showed me that it was crawling with them. I screamed and threw the bird down. Then I started to cry and sat down and watched Albert pick up the bird very carefully and examine its wing. "There's nothing you can do about this," he explained. "It's rotten. We'll have to kill it."

"But let it fly away," I whispered. "Perhaps it will get well after all."

"Why should it suffer?" said Albert. He took out his sheath-knife and held the bird by the head, pressing it down onto the raft. I stopped crying and watched, I just couldn't look away. Albert turned round so that he was between me and the gull. Then he cut right through its neck and let the head and the body of the gull slip into the water. When he turned round again, he was as white as a sheet.

"Look, there's blood!" I whispered and began to tremble all over. Then he rinsed the blood away.

"Don't get worked up about it," he said. "You see, it was much the best way."

He was so kind that I began to cry again, and now it was lovely to be able to cry. Everything was over and everything was alright.

Albert always put things right. Whatever happened, and however one behaved, it was always Albert who put things right.

He stood looking at me, worried and not understanding. "Don't be cross any longer," he said. "Look, the fog's lifting and the wind is changing."

Flotsam and Jetsam

IF THE WATER RISES, THERE'LL BE A STORM. IF IT FALLS very quickly and sharply, there might be a storm too. A ring around the sun may be dangerous. And a smoky, dark-red sunset bodes no good either. There are many more things like this, but I can't be bothered with them just now. If it's not one thing, then it's another.

In the end, Daddy couldn't put up with being uneasy about the weather and set off. He set the spritsail and said, "Now remember that one mustn't have a single unnecessary thing in a boat."

We sat still. We weren't allowed to read because that shows a lack of respect for the boat. You couldn't trail anything in the water, such as painters or boats of bark, because the pilots might see them. We gave the sand-bank a fairly wide berth, but not too narrow because that's asking for trouble, and not too wide because that looks too cautious and the pilots might see it. Then we were on our way.

There are lots of things to attend to in a boat. You have to watch out for the painter; otherwise it gets tangled round your feet and can pull you overboard. You might slip when going ashore and hit your head and drown. You can sail too close to the shore and get caught in the undertow. You can stay too far away from the shore and end up in Estonia in the fog. In the end you go aground and then everything really gets into a pickle. Although he thinks all the time about the things that might go wrong, Daddy loves great waves, particularly if they come from the south-west and get bigger and bigger.

Things turn out just as he said and the wind gets stronger and stronger. So now he doesn't need to be uneasy any longer but can be calm and cheerful while the wind blows.

'Alas and alack we're leaving the shore, Oh maiden so fair we'll see you no more.' We're living under the sprit-sail on Acre Island and the wind is getting stronger all the time.

The Hermansons and the Seaforths arrived a little later. They have no children. They put up their sail for the night next to ours. And there we all were in the storm. All the females rushed around putting things straight and all the men rolled huge stones and shouted to each other and pulled the boats higher up. When the evening came, Mummy wrapped me in a blanket. From under the sail one could see a triangle of heather and surf and the sky that got bigger or smaller as the sail flapped in the wind. All night the men went down to the shore to see that everything was as it should be. They pulled up the boats and measured the height of the water and estimated the strength of the wind out on the point. From time to time, Daddy came in to see whether we were still there and stuffed his pockets full of bread. He looked at me and knew that I was enjoying the storm just as much as he was.

Next morning we discovered a motorboat on the far side of the island. It lay there quite abandoned bumping up against the rocks; two planks had split and it was full of water. And they had had no oars with them. They hadn't even risked their lives trying to save the boat.

It's just as I have always said: you can never rely on a motor; it just breaks down. People who go out to sea might well bother themselves to learn something about it first. They have never seen a spritsail in their lives and go and buy boats with high gunnels and then leave them lying on the beach without any tar and so they get leaky and become a disgrace to the whole community.

We stood looking at the boat for a while and then went straight up the shore and looked in the clump of willows behind the rocks on the beach, and there it all was – two-gallon canisters like a silver carpet under the bushes as far as you could see and a little higher up they had tucked the brandy under some spruce trees. "Well," Daddy said. "Well! It can't be true."

All the men started to run all over the place and the females followed, with Mummy and me last, running as fast as we could.

On the lee-side Daddy and Mr Hermanson were talking to three soaking-wet fellows who were eating our sandwiches. The females and Mr Seaforth were standing a little way away. Then Daddy came up to us and said, "Now, this is what we're going to do. Hermanson and I will take them home because they have been drifting for three days without food and can hardly stand on their feet. If all goes well, each family will get four bottles and three canisters. Seaforth can't go with us as a matter of principle, because he's a customs man himself."

We sat in a row and watched them sail away. Sometimes you could get a glimpse of the boat but sometimes you couldn't see them at all.

Mrs Seaforth looked at Mr Seaforth and said: "Think carefully what you're doing."

"I'm thinking alright!" he answered. "Do you think this is easy for me? But I've made up my mind. I shan't take any notice of the whole thing, and I shan't accept a single bottle or a canister, either. In any case, I'm on holiday and I'm not the only one who's taking them home. And they've eaten my sandwiches, too. Jansson would understand what I mean."

When Daddy and Mr Hermanson came back, they were soaked to the skin and very cheerful, and immediately they came ashore they went to fetch the canisters. They took one each, but Seaforth didn't take one at all because he was being loyal to the coastguards.

"But they promised us four," said Mrs Hermanson. "And three bottles of brandy."

"That was while they were scared," said Daddy. "When we got them home they changed their minds, and said one canister for each family."

"That's three, then," said Mrs Hermanson. "And we can share the Seaforth's."

"That wouldn't be right," said Daddy. "There are principles involved in this. Two canisters, and that's all. Besides, the journey itself was worth something. Women don't understand these things."

We hid the canisters in the seaweed.

Towards evening the wind died down and we sailed home, each family going their own way. Then we put the canisters in the fish-cage. We said nothing, we kept quiet.

There are people who sell canisters that they have found and overcharge for them. That's no way to behave. Others row the canisters to the coastguard. It happened once in Pernby.

To buy a canister is like cheating the government, and anyway is too expensive, and one doesn't do that sort of thing. The only proper way is to find a canister and preferably save it at the risk of one's life. Such a canister is a source of satisfaction and does no harm to anybody's principles.

But a boat that has floated ashore or is just drifting is an entirely different matter. Boats are serious things. One has to search and search until one finds the owner even if it takes years to find him. It's just the same with fishing-nets that have broken loose and are drifting. They must go back to their owners. Everything else one is allowed to keep – logs, planks and pit-props and net-floats and buoys.

But the worst thing one can do is to take flotsam that has already been salvaged by someone else. That's unforgivable. If it has been piled up against a stone or collected in a neat pile with two stones on top of it, it is reserved. You can reserve it with two stones, but three are better. One stone is not to be relied on, because it might have got there by accident. There are people who take other people's piles, or even worse just take the best things from each pile. I know! If one has rescued a plank, one always recognises it again. And often one knows exactly who has been where one left it. But one says nothing about it afterwards, because that would be in bad taste, and in any case who told one to reserve things with stones instead of making two trips to row everything home?

What is right and what is wrong is a very sensitive matter. One could say a lot about it. For example, if you come across a boat floating all by itself with a cabinet in it full of canisters, it goes without saying that one searches for the owner of the boat and keeps the cabinet oneself, if it is a nice one. But how many canisters is one allowed to keep? There's a lot of difference between a canister in a boat, in the undergrowth, or in the water, or in a cabinet that is in a boat.

Once I found a boat made of bark that was called *Darling*. It was very beautifully made with a hold, rudders, a wheelhouse and cloth sails. But Daddy said I didn't have to find out who owned it.

Maybe nothing is so important, provided that it is small enough. At least, that's what I think.

High Water

ONE SUMMER THE BOATHOUSE WAS EMPTY BECAUSE Old Charlie was out fishing all the time. Mummy sat on our veranda and drew illustrations and sent them to town with the herring boat. From time to time she took a dip in the sea and then she went on drawing again.

Daddy looked at her and then he went and looked in the boathouse and in the end he went to town and fetched his modelling stand and box of clay, his armatures and his modelling tools. He turned the boathouse into a studio and everybody got interested in it and helped him. They tried to tidy up all Old Charlie's tools and wanted to clean the floor, but that they weren't allowed to.

Daddy got cross and then they understood that, for Daddy, the boathouse was a sacred place and not to be disturbed in any way. Nobody went down the field near the beach and the boats had to tie up at the herring jetty.

It was a very hot summer and the wind never blew.

Mummy drew and drew, and every time a drawing was cleaned up with a rubber she allowed herself to take a dip. I stood next to the table on the veranda and waited till she held up a drawing so that the Indian ink could dry faster and we both laughed because we were thinking what it was like in town when drawing was done at night and made you so tired that you felt sick. Then we ran down to the beach and jumped into the sea. When Old Charlie had people from town staying with him, I had to wear my knickers in the water.

Daddy was working in his new studio. He went there after he'd been fishing and had his breakfast. Daddy loves to go fishing. He gets up at four in the morning and takes his fishing-rod and goes and looks at the bleak fish in the bait box.

It was so hot in the bay that the bleak all died, and we put out the net almost every evening just off Sandy Island. We put a packet of crispbread for Daddy on the veranda every morning. He filled his pockets full and rowed out through the sound.

A mooring-stone is very important. One can look for hours without finding a really good one, as they have to be slightly oval and have a notch in the middle. In the morning Daddy goes fishing by himself. Nobody interferes with him and nobody says he mustn't. The lighting is wonderful then and the rocks look just as good as if Cavvy had painted them. One just sits and looks at the float, and one knows the fish will bite and when they'll bite. There's a rock underneath the water that has been named after Daddy; it's called Jansson's Rock and will be called that for ever and ever. Then one makes one's way home slowly, looking to see if there's smoke coming out of the chimney.

Nobody else likes fishing. But Mummy helps with the bag-net and sits at the helm and trails a trolling-spoon. She has no sense of where the right spots are, but that's something people are born with and it's seldom found in women.

Daddy went to his new studio after breakfast. It was just as hot every day and there was never any wind.

Daddy got more and more glum. He began to talk politics. Nobody went near the boathouse and we didn't bathe near there either, but went to the first bay instead.

The worst thing was the way in which Old Charlie's visitors behaved. They went out of their way to cut Daddy off and, when they saw him coming, addressed him as 'Sculptor' and asked him whether he had had any inspiration or not. I have never heard anything so tactless. They crept past the boathouse in an obvious way, putting their fingers up to their lips, whispering and nodding to one another and giggling, and naturally Daddy could see the whole performance through the window.

And the worst thing was that they suggested motifs to him. Mummy and I felt so terribly embarrassed for them, but what could we do?

Daddy became more and more glum and in the end he didn't speak to anyone at all. One morning he didn't even go fishing but stayed in bed staring at the ceiling with his lips pursed.

And it got hotter and hotter.

Then all of a sudden the water began to rise. We didn't notice it until the wind got up during the night. It all happened in half an hour. A mass of dry twigs and rubbish from the yard was blown against the window-panes and the storm roared through the forest, and it was so hot that one couldn't even bear to have a sheet over one in bed. The door was burst open and we ran out onto the steps and saw that there were white horses behind Red Rock, and then we saw the water glistening right up round the well and Daddy cheered up and shouted, "Well, I'll be damned! What weather!", and put his trousers on and was outside in a jiffy.

Old Charlie's visitors had been blown out onto the slope in their nightshirts and stood there all huddled together and had no idea at all what to do. But Mummy and Daddy went down to the beach and watched the jetty floating away towards Reed Island with all the boats push-ing and nudging each other as though they were alive, and the fish-cage had broken adrift and all the pit-props were floating out through the sound. It was marvellous!

The grass was under water, the sea was rising all the time, and the storm and the night made the whole land-scape look quite different.

Old Charlie ran to fetch the clothesline and Fanny stood there shouting and banging a tin can and her

white hair was flying in all directions. Daddy rowed out
to the jetty with a line and Mummy stood on the shore
holding it.

Everything lying on the slope below the house had
floated out to sea and the offshore wind was carrying it
out towards the sound and the wind was getting stronger
and stronger and the water was rising higher and higher.
I was shouting with glee, too, as I waded up and down
and felt the floating grass getting tangled round my legs.
I was trying to save planks and from time to time Daddy
ran past hauling logs and shouting: "What do you think
of this! The wind's getting stronger all the time!"

He flung a rope to the visitors and shouted: "Take
hold of this, damn you! We must get the jetty up into
the field! Do something! Don't just stand there!" And
the visitors hauled on the rope and were soaked to the
skin in their nightshirts and had no idea what fun the
whole thing was, which served them right.

In the end we saved everything that could be saved
and Mummy went into the house to make tea. I pulled
off my clothes and was wrapped in a blanket and
sat and watched Mummy lighting the fire. The
window-panes rattled and were quite dark and it
started to rain.

Then Daddy burst in and went into the kitchen and
shouted: "Damn it! Can you imagine what's happened!
The clay looks like porridge. It's a damned nuisance, but
there's nothing to be done about it!"

"How terrible," said Mummy, looking just as pleased
as Daddy.

"I've been down to the first bay," Daddy said, "and it's blowing hard down there and a whole load of logs is floating in. I've no time for tea now. I'll be back later."

"Alright," said Mummy. "I'll keep it warm."

Then Daddy went out again. Mummy poured out tea for us all. It was the best storm we had ever had.

Jeremiah

ONE YEAR TOWARDS AUTUMN A GEOLOGIST WAS LIVING in the pilot's hut. He couldn't speak either Finnish or Swedish; he just smiled and flashed his black eyes. He would look at people and immediately make them feel how surprised and happy he was to meet them at last and then he just walked on with his hammer and hammered a rock here and there. His name was Jeremiah.

He borrowed a boat to row out to the islands and Old Charlie stood and sniggered at Jeremiah because he rowed so miserably. One felt embarrassed for Jeremiah when he took to the water and Daddy wondered what the pilots thought when they saw him rowing.

It was very sensible of me to look after Jeremiah. He couldn't even tie a proper half-hitch – when he tried to, it looked more like some kind of bow. Sometimes he even forgot to tie the boat up. But it was because he didn't care about anything else in the world except stones. They didn't have to be pretty and round or odd in any way. He had ideas of his own about stones and they were quite different from anybody else's.

I never got in his way and I only showed him my collection of stones once. Then he put on such a great show of admiring them that I was embarrassed. He overdid things in the wrong way. But later on he learned better.

We walked along the beach, him in front and me behind. When he stopped, I stopped and stood still and watched while he hammered away, but I never came too close. He hadn't often got time for me. But sometimes when he turned round and caught sight of me he pretended to be terribly surprised. He bent forward and screwed up his eyes and tried to look at me through his magnifying glass, then shook his head as though it was impossible that anyone could be as tiny as I was. Then he saw me anyway and stepped backwards in surprise and pretended that he was holding something very, very small in his hands and we both started to laugh.

Sometimes he would draw both of us in the sand, one very tall and one very small, and once I was allowed to borrow his jersey when the wind got up. But otherwise he mostly hammered away at the rocks and forgot all about me. I didn't mind. I always walked behind him and in the morning I waited outside the pilots' hut until he woke up.

We played a game. I put a present on his doorstep and then hid myself, and when he came out he found

the present and was delighted. He puzzled over it and scratched his head and threw his arms in the air and then began to look for me. He looked in a rather stupid way, but that was all part of the game. He had to take a long time to find me and to discover how terribly tiny I was. I tried to make myself smaller and smaller so that he would be delighted. We hammered away at the rocks for many days together. Then it got cloudy and windy and rather cold, and then she came.

She had the same kind of hammer as Jeremiah and walked around hammering in exactly the same way as he did, and she couldn't speak Swedish or Finnish either. She lived in Old Charlie's sauna.

I knew that Jeremiah wanted to hammer on his own. He didn't want her to come with him but she just came. If one wants to collect stones, one should be allowed to do so on one's own. She could have looked for them on her own, but she didn't. She kept appearing from a different direction and always pretended to be surprised at meeting Jeremiah. But her game of pretending was phony and hadn't anything to do with us two.

I followed behind with Jeremiah's little box and stood waiting while he hammered away. I made sure that the boat was properly tied up. But of course we couldn't play our game of how tiny I was while she was there.

In the beginning she smiled at me, but in fact all she did was bare her teeth. I stared at her until she looked away and went on hammering. I followed them and stood waiting, and every time she turned round she looked at me and I never looked back at her. We froze because the wind blew right in our faces and the sun never shone. I could see that she was freezing cold and that she was afraid of the water. But she came in the boat too and she never let him go out to the islands by himself.

She sat in the stern and gripped the gunnels with both hands and I could see from them how scared she was. She pressed her knees tightly together and craned her neck and gulped. She didn't look at the waves but just stared at Jeremiah the whole time, and he rowed zigzag as best he could against the wind, and off they went together and got smaller and smaller.

I wasn't allowed to go with them in the boat any longer. They pretended that it was too small. It was a stout flat-bottomed boat and I could well have sat in the bows. Jeremiah knew it but he was afraid of her. I waited until I saw them set off and then come back to the bays. Then I would hide in the shelter of a rock and watch them, and wherever they came ashore I was there to meet them and tie up their boat.

I knew that nothing was fun any longer and couldn't be, but I followed them all the same. I couldn't stop following them, every day and all day until the evening, and I had my own food with me. But we didn't swap sandwiches any more. We kept ourselves to ourselves and we all sat at the same distance from each other and none of us said anything.

Then we would get up and walk along the shore. Once she stopped and stood still and waited for me without turning round. I stopped too, because her back took on a dangerous shape. And then she turned round and said something to me. It was the first time she had opened her mouth. At first I didn't understand. Then she said it again, over and over, very loud and in a shrill voice: "Go home! Go home, go home!" Somebody had taught her to say "Go home!" but it sounded queer.

I looked down at my feet and waited until she went on, and then I followed again.

But in the morning she wasn't there. So I put my present on the steps of the pilot's hut and hid. I could stay in hiding as long as they liked. Then Jeremiah came out onto the steps and found the present and was surprised. He began to search for me and I was terribly tiny; so tiny that I could have fitted into his pocket.

But gradually everything changed. I grew and he found me much too quickly. He wasn't at all surprised. At last the awful thing had happened: we were playing the game because we had started to play it and thought it was something too embarrassing to stop.

One day Jeremiah came out onto the steps and found his present. He threw his arms into the air as usual and clutched his head. But then he didn't take his hands away but held his head far too long. Then he came right up to the pine tree where I was hiding and stood in front of me and smiled and I could see he was baring his teeth just like she did and wasn't at all friendly. It was so awful that I just ran away.

I was ashamed for both our sakes all day. At three o'clock the sun came out and I went back to the bays.

They were in the third bay. He sat hammering and she was looking on a little way away. She wasn't cold any longer and had taken off her woolly cap and undone her hair – masses of it that fell all over the place while she was looking at him. Then she went closer and laughed and bent down to see what he was doing and her hair fell all over, him and he got scared and straightened up and bumped her nose. I think it was her nose. She nearly fell over, so Jeremiah took a firm hold of her and for an instant they looked like paper dolls. Then she began to speak very rapidly and Jeremiah held on to her and listened.

He was so far away from me that I had to shout so that he would hear me, and I shouted for all I was worth. But he just walked away and she was left standing there staring at me and I stared back. I stared and stared at her until I had stared her into little pieces and I thought, 'You're big and scraggy like a carthorse and nobody can hunt for you in the grass and you couldn't hide anywhere because you can be seen the whole time and you can't surprise anybody and make them feel good! You have completely spoilt our game for no reason at all because you can't play games yourself! O alas and alack! No one wants your presents. He doesn't want them. You're nobody's surprise, and you can't understand because you're not an artist!' And so I went a little closer and humiliated her by saying the most terrible thing of all: "Amateur! You're an amateur! You're not a real artist!"

She stepped backwards and screwed up her face. Then I daren't look at her any longer because it's an awful shame to see a grown-up person cry. So I looked at the ground and waited a long time. I heard her walk away. When I looked up she had gone.

Jeremiah was on the point hammering away. So I went back to the pilots' hut and took back my present. It was a very beautiful skeleton of a bird, and quite white. Mummy gave me a box just the right size and I took the skeleton with me when I went back to town. It's very unusual to come across the skeleton of a bird which is the right chalky-white colour.

The Spinster Who Had An Idea

WEEK AFTER WEEK SHE SAT MAKING STEPS WITH CEMENT outside Old Charlie's little house. But it was very slow work. They had to be terribly pretty and unlike any other steps in the whole world. They were to be her present to us for being allowed to live in our attic.

She woke up earlier and earlier in the morning. We heard her squeaking terribly slowly down the stairs because she was so afraid of waking us up. Then she started moving her buckets and her stones outside the veranda just as slowly, and occasionally we heard a little clanking sound and then a scraping noise and a thud and a splash, and in the end we were wide awake and lay waiting for the next cautious movement.

Sometimes she creaked across the veranda to fetch something she had forgotten and opened the door, put her fingers to her lips and whispered: "Sleep soundly, Shh! Don't worry about me." And then she smiled sadly and secretively. She was tall and thin and had anxious eyes set close together and she had reached that certain age. What exactly that certain age was, and why she had reached it, no one would tell me, but in any case life wasn't easy for her and the steps were all she cared about. That's why we admired what she was doing so much.

When we came out on the veranda she shouted: "No! no! no! no! wait a moment!" She jumped to her feet quickly and began to haul up a plank and lifted one end of it onto the threshold and the other end onto a box. While we were balancing ourselves on the plank, she looked terrified and implored: "I've only just cemented it! Do be careful and please don't tread anywhere near it!"

Then Daddy picked up the plank so she could go on cementing and she thanked him much too profusely for his help.

Day after day she was on her knees trying to fit stones into the cement, and round her she had buckets of cement and water, and sand and rags and trowels and small sticks and spades. The stones had to be flat and smooth and pretty in colour. They lay there arranged in piles according to a very well thought-out plan and on no account were they to get mixed up. The smallest stones were red and white and were kept separately in a box.

We started to get out through the bedroom window, but only when she wasn't looking. Once when

Mummy was carrying some pails of water over the plank, she spilled a few drops and a very important part of the concrete was spoilt. Then we started lifting the pails of water through the window, too.

I knew I wasn't allowed to help her because she wanted to play on her own. So I just stood and looked on.

She had begun with the small red and white stones and was poking a long row of them into the cement. It was supposed to be some kind of saying, and every time a little stone got into the wrong place she gave a little wail.

"Don't you like playing?" I asked.

She didn't understand what I meant. "It's so difficult," she said. "You mustn't look!" So I went away.

She had thought that she would put 'Bless All Those Who Cross This Threshold' on the steps but she forgot to measure it. So when at last she got to the end there wasn't enough room for 'Threshold'. 'Thresh' was all that she could fit in.

"You ought to have measured it before you started," Daddy said. "And used a bit of string to keep it straight. I could have shown you how to do it."

"It's easy to say that when it's too late!" she cried. "I don't think you care one bit about my steps! I know you climb in the window just to show me I'm in the way!"

"Dammit, what other way should we go, with your pots and pans all over the place," Daddy said.

Then she started to cry and rushed up to the attic. Daddy was left standing there looking miserable, and said, "Oh damn."

The steps never really got finished. She lost interest in them and moved all her things down to the big rock instead, in order to cement stones in the big tub. The plank was taken away. But the hole in the concrete where she had started to cry was still there staring at us.

All the next day she emptied the big tub with buckets. When she had almost reached the bottom, she borrowed the scoop. Then she used a tea cup and a sponge. But right at the bottom there were nasty creepy-crawly things living in the slime and she was afraid of them although she felt sorry for them. It was so awful getting them up from the bottom she was on the point of screaming, but she said, "It's got to be done," and she carried them over to another tub, and in between tea cups she put her arms in the sea and waved them about while her tears fell into the water.

When the tub was quite empty, she started to put rows of stones at the bottom and then cemented them. She twisted and turned each stone in order to get it to fit but she couldn't do it. She tried one stone after another but none of them would fit. Then she noticed that I was standing by the woodpile. "You mustn't look," she shouted. So I went away again.

She looked for new stones in the bay, but they were either the wrong shape or the wrong colour. But the hardest thing was to get the stones clean when they were finally in place. She washed them and wiped them and rinsed her rag again and again, but when the stone was dry it still had a little fleck of cement on it and then she had to start from the beginning again.

And in the winter the tub froze at the bottom and the whole thing cracked. It was very difficult being a spinster.

When she came back the following summer I was terribly afraid that everything would go wrong for her again. We had filled the hole on the steps with sand and poured a little milk into the tub so that she wouldn't be able to see how awful the bottom looked. But she wasn't interested in cement any longer. She had brought with her a whole suitcase full of her scrapbooks with glossy cut-out pictures and she put them to soak in the wash-tub. Then she peeled off all the glossy pictures and laid them out to dry on the slope. It was a beautiful calm Sunday and the slope was dotted with pictures of roses and angels by the thousand and she was happy again and carried them up to her room in the attic. It was such a relief to see that she was happy!

"Things seem a bit better this time," Mummy said.

But Daddy said, "Do you think so? I'm not so sure, but as usual I'm not saying anything."

And she started sticking boxes together. She sat in her room in the attic making little boxes with lots of little compartments, which she covered with glossy pictures both on the inside and on the outside. The glossy pictures stuck straight away and kept their colour and didn't have to fit because she stuck them on top of each other.

The room in the attic was full of paper and pots of paste and boxes and big piles of glossy pictures that one wasn't allowed to touch. She sat down in the middle of it all, sticking and sticking, and in the end the pile of scrap paper reached up to her knees. But she never put anything in the boxes and never gave any of them away.

"Are they always going to be empty?" I asked.

She looked at the box she was making and didn't answer. Her long face had an anxious look and there was a glossy picture sticking to her fringe.

I got fed up with her because she wasn't happy. I don't like it when people find life difficult. It gives me a bad conscience and then I get angry and begin to feel that they might as well go somewhere else.

But Granny liked her because she had been a good customer at the button shop and they used to read Allers' *Family Magazine* together during the winter.

Granny had a lot of little boxes with lots of compartments, but at least she put buttons in them. While Granny's button business was a glorious success, each kind of button was kept separate, but when the business went bust the buttons got into the wrong compartments, which was actually much more fun.

Before the police came to the shop, Granny managed to rescue a lot of button boxes, which she hid under her skirts just as she had hidden guns during the 1918 war. She also rescued tons of Allers' *Family Magazines* and little porcelain dogs and velvet pin cushions and a quantity of nightcaps and silk ribbons, and then she sighed and said, "Bless me! Now we shall have to draw crosses on the ceiling again!" And she carried everything to Daddy's and Mummy's studio.

Mummy hid all the Allers' *Family Magazines* but Granny and I found them, particularly the ones with the whole-page pictures of sad things. A Young Witch Being Led to the Stake. A Heroine's Death.

And every copy of the magazine was kept for the spinster. Granny and she used to read them in secret in the bedroom. Once she came to read Allers' *Family Magazine* on the worst possible day she could have picked. Daddy was busy making a plaster cast. And it was a particularly large and difficult one that had to be made in sections.

The plaster was already mixed so, as you know, it was a question of seconds. You mustn't touch it and you must hardly breathe. I should never have dreamed of going into the studio just then. Mummy and Daddy were standing ready with their plastering clothes on and the whole floor was covered with brown paper.

And just then she came in and said: "Hallo! Hallo! Something's going on here, I can see. Don't let me disturb you!" I was standing behind the curtains and watching. She went straight up to the tub of plaster and poked a finger in it and said, 'Plaster! How funny, and just now when I'm particularly interested in plaster!"

Mummy said: "We're working." And Daddy looked ready to murder somebody. I was so frightened and embarrassed that I climbed up onto my bunk. I was sure that Daddy would throw clay at her, because that's what he always does when he's angry. But the only thing I could hear was the soft slapping sound of wet plaster. They had started casting. She babbled away the whole time without realising that she was interrupting an almost sacred ceremony.

Granny came out of the bedroom for a moment, looked terrified and went back inside. After a while I ventured down. By that time she had got an overall on and was standing by the window with both hands in a little bowl of plaster.

"Now it's going hard!" she shouted. "What shall I do next?"

And, instead of hitting her on the head, Daddy went up to her and showed her what to do. I looked at Mummy. She grinned and shrugged her shoulders. The spinster had cut out a picture from Allers' *Family Magazine* and put it face down on a saucer.

"Have you greased the saucer properly?" Daddy asked severely.

"Yes, yes," she said. "Just as you said."

"Well, pour it on," said Daddy. "But don't put your finger in it."

She poured the plaster into the saucer and Daddy took the putty knife and made the whole thing even. Then he said, "Do you want a hook too?"

"Yes, yes," she whispered, and was so happy that she drew her breath as she spoke. "It's to hang on the wall."

Daddy sniffed and went up to the reel of steel wire and cut off a bit. He made a loop and stuck it in the plaster on one side. "Don't touch it," he said. "Leave it to dry."

"You are kind," she breathed and the tears came to her eyes. "I shall come back tomorrow and bring my glossy cut-out pictures with me. They will be even more beautiful."

And she did, too!

All the time the plaster-casting was going on, she stood at the workbench and put glossy cut-outs into a saucer and poured plaster on them and put a loop at one end, just as Daddy had taught her to do. A whole row of plaster pictures lay on the bench, each with a big bright glossy cut-out in the middle. The pictures curved beautifully over the chalky-white plaster and had no spots on them at all because she got better and better at it all the time.

She was beside herself with joy. Granny came in and praised her. She gave each of us a picture and she hung Daddy's on the studio wall.

I didn't know what to think. The plaster pictures were really the most beautiful things I had ever seen, but they weren't Art. One couldn't respect them at all. Actually one should really have despised them. It was a terrible thing to do to make such pictures in Daddy's studio and, what's more, whilst a plaster cast was being made.

The worst thing was that she didn't even look at the statue standing there waiting to be touched up and given its patina, but just babbled on about her own pictures. The whole workbench was full of them and looked like a cake shop.

In the end she was given a big bag of plaster, and all the pictures were packed up in a box and she took the lot and went home and disappeared.

"What a relief!" said Mummy, and began to clean the floor. "Now you can take it down."

Daddy took the spinster's plaster plaque off the wall and looked at it and sniffed. I looked at him and thought, 'Now I must take mine down too.' I waited to see what he was going to do. For a moment he held it over the rubbish bin. Then he went over to the bookcase and shoved the plaque behind some early statuettes of his on the top shelf. You could only just see a little bit of the glossy picture.

I climbed up onto my bunk and took my picture off the nail. I put it behind a candlestick on the bookcase and stepped backwards to have a look. It didn't look right. So I pulled the picture forward a bit, just enough so that the candlestick hid a couple of forget-me-nots. It couldn't be helped that the glossy cut-out picture was really very beautiful and, to tell the truth, for me it wasn't at all profane.

The Boat and Me

WHEN I WAS TWELVE I GOT A ROWING BOAT OF MY OWN. It was two metres thirty long and clinker-built. When they asked me its name I said it's just called the boat. I had a plan for the boat and me: to row round the whole of Pellinge archipelago, uninhabited rocks and all, both the inner and outer parts, sort of encircle the lot and then it would be done. I don't know why it was important. The trip could take me twenty-four hours, so it was a good idea to take a sleeping-bag, but otherwise nothing but hard bread and fruit juice. As Dad says, you should never keep a single inessential object in your boat.

The start was fixed for the twentieth of August and it had to be kept absolutely secret.

I don't know how it was that Mum got wind of the project; maybe she noticed I'd taken the sleeping-bag out of the tent. She didn't say anything but somehow she let me know she knew about it and that she was on my side as far as deceiving Dad went. He would never have let me go. And I'm pretty sure Mum would never have managed to deceive her own father, who never let her sleep in a tent or even wear a sailor-suit collar. A terrible century.

Anyway, the boat and I were ready to start. The wind had been in the south-west for a couple of days, blowing the waves in and making them long. The boat was in high water, which reached up to the grass line, and when I launched her the keel slid out as if over velvet. As soon as she reached the sea she met the swell by the shore, but I held her steady by the gunwale and waited. The sky was white and empty as it usually is before sunrise and the gulls were alive in the heavens. Presently Mum hurried up with a cardigan over her nightdress, bringing sandwiches and a bottle of appleade: "Quick," she said, "Get going before he wakes!"

Departures are seldom what you expect.

We met heavy seas, there was a direct tailwind and, struggling to keep my balance, I pressed my feet against the floor and made good speed; Mum stood a long time waving from the shore.

Dad never waves at sea; it's something you should never do unless you're in distress.

I was taking the waves stern on but very soon realised this was a mistake: we needed to turn completely round pretty damn quick so as to be able to ride over them, so I waited till we were in a suitable trough, then drove the left oar straight down and pulled like mad on the right one, and in a moment we had wheeled round and the motion of the sea had taken charge of us as if it was entirely the obvious thing to happen.

While we were running on before the wind towards the outermost promontory, it occurred to me that the sea really needs a boat on it to be in control – I mean to be greater than everything else. Maybe it needs islands too, so long as they're small ones. And why not a gull in the sky? So long as it's cloudless, naturally.

And then the sun rose and shone right into my eyes and transformed the spray into pink roses, and we raced onwards and rounded the promontory until suddenly we were in the lee. It was quiet there. Of course you could hear the sea, but it seemed a long way off because now the wind was roaring through the forest nearby. Here by the sheltered shallows the forest stretches right down to the rocks on the shore, with the small islands sailing around like floating bouquets and everything's completely green – I know, I've been here before.

I bailed the boat, even though she'd hardly taken in any water, then we let ourselves run on for a bit.

This is where the summer birds live, the carefree people Dad despises. They wake late in the day in their summer-houses and go down to the sea on their rickety white-painted landing-stages with their nearby saunas and jump into their flashy high-powered metal motorboats.

Dad despises metal boats. He says these young toffs and their girls are nothing short of criminal; they use twenty horsepower just for pleasure, putting everyone else's lives at risk, not to mention the professional fishermen's nets.

Of course, I remember. The girl always sitting in the bows as far forward as she could, tanned and happy with her hair flying in the wind, loving the thrill of speed! As they race past she waves to me – but that was an awful long time ago.

I rowed on. It looked likely to be a very hot day and there was thunder in the air.

Gradually the shallows filled with people, travelling and fishing and bathing, delighting in that summer world which is like nothing else, with small children milling about off every shore on rafts and in canoes – when all of a sudden one of those flashy motor-boats drove straight through with bow waves like rainbows and the toff at the wheel shouted, "Hi! Want a tow?"

It was beneath me even to favour him with a glance.

Here came another. I rowed like mad and as it hissed past I saw the girl with flying hair in the bows and she waved to me.

I rowed on.

It wasn't the right girl, I knew that. But I could have waved even so – though probably I wouldn't have. Did these people in the shallows have any idea how stupid they were? Probably not. Was I being unfair to them? I expect I was.

Never mind. I rowed on and came near the narrow gap where the shallows open to the sea, after which the small islands thinned out and it became cooler.

Now I was getting near the most important part of my trip and I had to stop and think. I dropped the anchor-stone overboard, with the line secured to the rowlock. There seemed no need to sleep but I took out Mum's sandwiches. They were each separately wrapped in greaseproof paper, and on the outside of each she'd written 'cheese', 'sausage', etc., except that on one she'd put 'Long Live Freedom'. Silly. So I just ate hardbread and opened her appleade and watched the moon, which was about to climb the sky. It was still large and looked like a pickled apricot. The road from the moon stretched straight out to the boat and now you could hear the sea properly again.

This is the turning point, this is exactly where the way back begins and I'll be able to draw my journey on the coastal chart in a bold loop like a lassoo thrown round an archipelago! Now I'm coming to the creeks that face the sea, the uninhabited places that are my secret territory because I know them better than anyone and love them best.

I come here when I'm feeling lonely and especially when it's blowing, which it does most of the time. There are five creeks and six headlands with not even a shack as far as the eye can see (the pilot's cottage doesn't count). I go slowly, hugging the shore, into each creek and out round each headland; I mustn't miss anything out because it's a ritual. Naturally I must salvage anything that may have washed up on shore and secure it with a couple of stones but that has nothing to do with the ritual – everyone rescues flotsam without even thinking about it. Now I'm about to see my territory from the sea for the first time, that's important.

I pulled up the anchor-stone and rowed straight out into the path of the moon. Of course the moon's path is lovely as a picture in calm weather, but when it's rough it's even more beautiful, all splinters and flakes from precious stones like sailing through a sea set with diamonds!

And at that very moment Dad turned up, I knew it was him because I recognised his Penta. So he'd found me, and now it was just a question of whether he was angry or relieved or both, and should I let him have the first word or not – and then he turned off the motor and came alongside and grabbed the gunwale and said hello.

I said hello.

"Climb over," said Dad. "We'll take her in tow, and now I'm going to ask you once and for all: why do you have to worry your mother like this!?" He fixed the stern line, adding: "The way you're behaving is almost criminal." Then he started up the Penta, which made it impossible for either of us to add another word.

I sat in the bows. The boat danced after us as light as a hind and didn't take in a single drop of water.

I knew Dad enjoyed driving the Penta on the open sea, so I left that to him and concentrated first and foremost on my own territory, which I could now see from the sea. The further from it we went, the more I realised that seen from the sea it was nothing but an extremely boring strip of Finnish coastline, which no one else would ever be the least bit interested in seeing, which was fine by me: they could all stay away if they had no idea what beauty was!

I took off my cap and loosed my hair to the wind and thought of other things.

Dad had found the sandwiches and eaten them.

It was a very beautiful night. He began playing and showing off among the waves; every so often he looked at me but I pretended not to notice. It was beginning to get light; outside our home creek, he brushed Hällsten in a tight clever curve, but kept the tow-rope permanently slack so the boat had time to reach the shore sedately. When we came near the hill, Dad said: "Never do this again, just so you know." We said goodnight. It was getting steadily lighter; the sky was big and white, as it usually is before sunrise.

PART III

Travelling Light

The Squirrel

ONE WINDLESS DAY IN NOVEMBER, NEAR SUNRISE, SHE saw a squirrel at the landing place. It was sitting motionless near the water, scarcely visible in the half-light, but she knew it was a real live squirrel and she hadn't seen a living thing for a long time. You can't count gulls: they're always leaving; they're like wind over waves and grass.

She put on her coat over her nightshirt and sat down by the window. It was cold, with a cold that stood still in the four-walled room with its four windows. The squirrel didn't move. She tried to remember everything she knew about squirrels. The wind carries them on pieces of wood from island to island. And then the wind drops, she thought with a touch of cruelty. The wind dies or changes direction and they drift out to sea, it turns out to be not at all what they expected. Why do squirrels go sailing? Are they curious or just hungry? Are they brave? No. Just ordinary and stupid. She got up and went for her binoculars, and when she moved the cold crept inside her coat. She found it difficult to adjust the binoculars, so she laid them on the window-ledge and waited a little longer. The squirrel continued to sit at the landing place doing nothing, just sitting there. She watched it intently and, finding her comb in the pocket of her coat, combed her hair slowly while she waited.

Now the squirrel came up the hill, very quickly, ran forward towards the cottage and stopped suddenly. She studied the animal closely and critically. It was sitting upright with its paws hanging down, occasionally jerking its body in a nervous and apparently unmotivated move-ment, a sort of crawling leap. It dashed round the corner. She went to the next window, the one facing east, then to the south one. She could see right across the island from shore to shore, there were no trees or bushes in the way; she could see everything that came and went. Unhurrying, she went to the fireplace to light the fire.

First, two pieces of plank at the sides. Over them, a crosswork of kindling, amongst the kindling birch bark, and on top of that some long-burning wood. Once the wood was alight she began to dress, slowly and methodically.

She always dressed at sunrise, warmly and with anticipation, pulling on sweaters and buttoning moleskin trousers round her broad midriff, and when she had got into her boots and pulled down her earflaps she would usually sit in front of the fire in an inviolable state of wellbeing, completely still and without a thought in her head while the fire warmed her knees. She met each new day in the same way, waiting sternly for winter.

Autumn by the sea had not turned out to be the autumn she'd expected. There had been no storms. The island was withering peacefully, its grass rotting in the rain and the hill turning slippery with dark algae which reached far above the waterline as November became increasingly grey. Nothing had happened before the squirrel came ashore. She went to the mirror above the chest of drawers and detected on her upper lip a delicate latticework of little vertical wrinkles she'd never noticed before. Her face was an undefinable grey-brown like the November earth; squirrels become grey-brown in winter but they don't lose their colour, they only get a new skin. She set the coffee on the fire and said: "Whatever else, squirrels have no talent." The thought calmed her.

She mustn't be hasty. The animal needed time to get used to the island and most of all to the house, and to discover that the house was merely a motionless grey object. But of course a house, a room with four windows, isn't really motionless; the person moving inside it must seem a sharp, threatening silhouette. How would a squirrel understand the movements it sees in a room? How, seen from the outside, do movements in an empty room look? All she could do was move very slowly and in absolute silence. The prospect of living an entirely silent life seemed tempting, if she could achieve it voluntarily and not merely because the island was silent.

On the table lay paper in orderly white sheaves, always placed in the same way with pens beside them.

Any sheets of paper she'd already written on lay hidden against the surface of the table, because if words lie face down there's a chance they might change during the night; you may suddenly come to see them with a new eye, perhaps with a rapid flash of insight. It is conceivable.

It was possible the squirrel might stay overnight. It was possible it might stay through the winter.

She very slowly crossed the floor to the corner cupboard and opened its doors. The sea was restless today; everything was restless. She stood still holding the cupboard doors open while she tried to remember what she'd come to fetch. And as usual she had to go back to the fire to remember. Sugar. And then she remembered not sugar, not any more, because sugar made her fat. These delayed acts of remembering depressed her; she let go and her thoughts ran on, and sugar led to dogs and she wondered what if it had been a dog that had come ashore at the landing place, but she pushed the thought away and cut it out of her mind; it was a thought that diminished the squirrel's importance.

She began sweeping, painstaking and calm. She liked sweeping. It was a peaceful day, a day without dialogue. There was nothing to defend or accuse anyone of; everything had been cut out, all those words that could have been other words or might simply have been out of place and have led to great changes. Now there was nothing but a warm cottage full of morning light, herself sweeping and the friendly sound of coffee beginning to simmer. The room with its four windows simply existed and justified itself; it was safe and had nothing to do with any place where you could shut anything in or leave anything out. She drank her coffee and thought about nothing at all, resting.

A mean thought passed through her head: so much fuss about a squirrel, there are millions of them, they're not particularly interesting. One, a single specimen, has happened to come here. I must be careful, I'm exaggerating everything at the moment, perhaps I've been alone too long. But it was only a passing thought, a knowing observation that anyone at all might have made. She put down the cup. Three gulls were sitting on the promontory, all facing the same way. Now she was feeling a bit unwell again; it was too hot in front of the fire – she always felt ill after her morning coffee. She needed her little tot of Madeira, the only thing that helped.

That's how a day starts: light the fire, get dressed, sit in front of the fire. Sweep up, coffee, morning Madeira, wind the clock, brush your teeth, have a look at the boat, measure the height of the water. Cut firewood, worktime Madeira. Then comes the main body of the day. Not till sundown do the rituals begin again. Sundown Madeira, take in the flag, see to the slop-pail, light the lamp, food. Then comes the whole evening. Every day must be written up before dark, including the height of the water, the direction of the wind and the temperature, and the shopping list on the doorpost: *new batteries, stockings but not knitted, all kinds of vegetables, embrocation, spare glass shade for lamp, saw-blade, butter, Madeira, sheer-pins for the propeller.*

She went to the wardrobe to fetch her morning medi-
cine. The Madeira was kept furthest in, closest to the
chill from the hall, she liked it cold. A bottle must have
its fixed place. The steps down to the cellar under the
floor were precipitous and awkward and she thought it
cowardly to hide bottles outside the house. There weren't
many bottles left. Sherry didn't count: it made you sad
and wasn't good for the stomach.

The morning light had grown stronger, and the wind
was still calm. She ought to catch the bus in to town to
get more Madeira. Not yet but soon, before the weather
got too cold. The motor was giving trouble; she ought to
try and do something about it, but it wasn't the sparking-
plug this time. She understood nothing about the motor
beyond the sparking-plug and sheer-pin. Now and then
she emptied the tank and filtered the petrol through
cloth. She had leaned the motor against the wall of the
house and covered it with a bag, and there it stood now.
Of course, one could row. But the boat was heavy and
tended to veer into the wind. It was too far. The whole
subject was disagreeable; she shut it out.

She noiselessly opened the screw-top, holding the
bottle between her knees and pressing the stopper against
her palm as she turned it, coughing the moment the
metal sleeve broke and filling her glass with the bottle
held at right angles before she remembered none of
this was necessary. It was her morning Madeira anyway,
which she had a right to because she wasn't feeling well.
She carried the glass into the cottage and stood it on
the table; the wine shone a deep red against the light

from the window. When the glass was empty she hid it behind the tea-caddy. She went to the window and tried to see the squirrel. She moved very softly from window to window waiting for it to appear. The wine had warmed her, the fire was burning in the fireplace, she moved round anticlockwise rather than clockwise, very calmly. The wind was still quiet and the sea and the sky joined together in a grey nothing, but the hill was black from the night's rain. Now the squirrel came. It came as if to reward her for having been calm and having cut every-thing else out of her life. The little animal leapt over the hill in soft S-shaped curves, straight across the island and down to the water; now it was sitting at the landing place again. It's going away, she thought. 'There's nowhere to stay here, nothing to eat, no other squirrels, and the storms will come and then it'll be too late.'

She got down laboriously on her knees and pulled out the bread bin from under the bed. Animals know when it's time to move on, like rats leaving a sinking ship, swimming or sailing away from what's doomed. She crept over the hill, moving as carefully as she could, and broke small pieces from the hardbread and put them in crevices. Now it had seen her. It ran down to the water's edge and sat there motionless; all she could see was a speck, a silhouette, but its outline radiated watchfulness and mistrust; now it's going to leave, now it's afraid! She went on breaking the bread as quickly as she could, faster, faster, hitting it with her fists, snapping it against her knees and throwing the pieces about on the ground, then scurried back into the cottage on all fours and over to the window. The landing place was empty. She waited an hour, went from window to window. The breeze was marking the sea with dark streaks; it was difficult to see whether there was anything moving out there, any float-ing object or swimming animal. She could only see birds that were resting like white spots on the water before flying up and gliding away out over the promontory. Then the streaks made by the breeze intensified and she could see nothing at all; her eyes grew tired and moist. She was desperately sorry for the squirrel and for herself too. She was a fool and had made herself ridiculous.

It was time for her worktime Madeira. Never mind cleaning her teeth, cutting firewood and measuring the height of the water, all that; she must be careful not to grow pedantic. She took out her glass, filled it quickly and carelessly, and, after emptying it, put it on the table and stood still and listened. The quality of the silence had changed, it was blowing a bit now, a steady easterly wind. The morning light had vanished from the room, the early glow of expectation and opportunity, now the daylight was ordinary and grey, a new day already partly used up, a bit soiled with wrong thoughts and point-less actions. Everything to do with the squirrel seemed unpleasant and embarrassing, so she cut it out.

She stood in the middle of the room in the warmth of her worktime Madeira and knew: 'This is only a moment, a moment that will pass quickly, I must use it or make it new.' All her pans hung in a row above the fireplace, all her books stood side by side on their shelves and all her nautical instruments were on the wall, decorative objects without which it might be hard to survive on a winter sea. Though there were never any storms. In other circumstances she might have been able to write to someone: *We're in a number eight force gale. I'm working. The salmon float is banging against the wall outside and waves have covered the windows with spray. No. The windows have been blinded by salt water. Covered with spray from... blinded. Spray from the breakers is crashing over... Dear Mr K. We're in the midst of a number eight gale...*

'There is no storm. It's just blowing, spiteful and stubborn, or there's a shiny swollen sea licking endlessly at the shore. If the wind gets any stronger, I ought to have a look at the boat, and when I've done that I'll deserve an extra Madeira which needn't be counted in with the others.'

At this point the squirrel came. A little rustle, a scurrying along the cottage wall, then its claws scraped the window and she saw its watchful face, its snout moving spasmodically with ridiculous little twitches, its eyes like glass balls. For a moment it was really close, then the window was empty again. She started laughing, 'So you're still here, you devil...' Now she needed wind, any kind of wind, no matter what, so long as it stood out from the mainland and the big islands. She tapped the barometer and tried to see whether it was sinking. Her specs weren't where they usually were; she could never find them, but surely it would say unsettled as it usually did. She must get the weather, the weather report; then she remembered that the batteries in the radio were dead. Never mind, no problem, the squirrel had stayed.

She went to the list by the door and added: *Squirrel food*. What do they eat, oats, macaroni, beans? She could cook oatmeal porridge. The two of them would adjust to each other. But it mustn't grow tame, at all costs not too tame, she would never try and get it to eat out of her hand, come into the cottage, or come when she called. The squirrel mustn't become a domestic animal, a responsibil- ity, a conscience – it must be allowed to stay wild. They would each live their own lives and just watch each other and recognise each other, be tolerant and respect each other, and otherwise get on with their own activities in full freedom and independence.

She didn't give a damn about that dog any more. Dogs are dangerous, they mirror everything, instantly, they're superficial, compassionate beasts. A squirrel's better.

They prepared themselves to winter on the island, they got used to one another and developed habits in common. After her morning coffee she would lay out bread on the hill and sit at her window to watch the squirrel eat. She'd decided the animal couldn't see her through the glass pane and that it probably wasn't particularly intelligent, but she persisted in moving slowly and had become used to sitting still for long periods, hours even, while she watched the squirrel's movements and thought about nothing in particular. Sometimes she talked to it but never when it was within hearing. She wrote about it, imagining things and observing things, and drew paral- lels between the two of them. Occasionally she wrote offensive things about the squirrel; insolent accusations that she regretted later and crossed out.

The unsettled weather grew steadily colder. Every day, immediately after she'd measured the height of the water, she would go up the hill to the place where she kept a great pile of wood. She would pick out several planks, and a section of trunk perhaps, and saw and chop them into firewood, carefully and not without skill. Doing this she was as strong and sure of herself like when she sat in front of the fire at sunrise, ready dressed, still as a statue and without a thought in her head. When she'd finished cutting the wood, she would carry it down to the cottage and arrange it carefully in the fireplace, every chunk and fragment of plank, into compact and elegant triangles and squares, broad and narrow rectangles and semicircles, creating a puzzle, a perfect intarsia. She'd collected the winter firewood herself.

The wind changed constantly. The boat lines had to be lengthened and moored again. Waking in the night she lay listening and worrying about the boat, worrying it might be banging against the hillside. In the end she pulled it up out of the water. But she woke all the same, thinking of high water and storms. She must haul it higher up, on rollers. One morning she went to the lumber-pile and chose a smooth slender trunk to cut rollers from; she took hold of it and pulled. A log fell down on the far side and there was a quick movement as of a living thing; something slipped out and vanished in a lightning movement of fear. She let go of the trunk and stepped back. Of course, this was where it lived.

It had made itself a home and now its home had been destroyed. "But I didn't know," she argued in her own defence. "How could I have known!"

She let the trunk lie, ran back to the cottage to get some wood-wool and flung back the trapdoor to the cellar, only remembering her pocket torch when she was already down in the darkness, she always forgot it. Jars, cartons, boxes – had she ever had any wood-wool? Perhaps it was glass-wool she'd had and that wouldn't be any good for a squirrel – glass fibre, if glass-wool is made of glass... She groped along the shelves and felt again that uncertainty which in many ways afflicts everything that exists, a constant stumbling between forgetfulness and knowledge, recollection and ideas, rows and rows of boxes and you never know which are empty... 'Now I must pull myself together. The box I'm looking for is full of muddle and confusion, things for the motor, a cardboard box under the stairs.' She found it and began to pull out the mess it contained in long recalcitrant tangles, opposition and darkness becoming an image of the night's dreams, dreams that she must hurry and that it was almost too late. She tore at the tough hostile material and knew: 'I'm not going to make it.'

It was no longer just a matter of the squirrel, but of everything that can ever be too late. In the end she took the whole box in her arms and tried to get it up the cellar steps. It was too big. It became wedged in the trapdoor hatch. She pushed with her shoulders and neck, the box broke and the confused tangle fell out over the floor. Now she only had seconds left. She ran up the hill, stumbled and ran on, crept round the woodpile and pushed the tangled waste in everywhere where it would be easy to find and couldn't get wet. "There you are! Build! Make yourself a home!" Now it was obvious she could do nothing more. Her large body had never felt so heavy; she manoeuvred herself slowly down into a sheltered crevice in the side of the rock, pulled up her legs to sleep and put the squirrel altogether out of her mind. She was safe and private, totally self-contained inside her sweaters, boots and raincoat, cocooned deep in a warm space of damp wool and easy conscience.

After midday it began to rain. She was woken by an awareness that had matured during her sleep, about the winter firewood, the wood she would need every day right through the winter. Constant ant-like expeditions up the hill, to saw and chop her way deeper and deeper down into the pile, an obstinate and implacable enemy getting nearer and nearer and opening new apertures of cold and light around a seduced and accursed squirrel lying in its home of tangled waste.

They must divide the winter firewood between them, that was absolutely clear. One pile for the squirrel and one for her and it must be arranged at once. Her body was stiff after her sleep but entirely calm, because there was only one thing for her to do. She went straight to the woodpile, heavy as a house. She dragged down logs, clutched hold of one and staggered down the hill with it towards the cottage. The hill was slippery, her boots slid on the moss, but she kept going to the bottom and offloaded the log against the wall of the house, turned and went up the hill again. The logs had to be carried, not rolled. A rolling log is an uncontrollable and arbitrary force that crushes everything in its path. The logs must be carried, carefully, to the exact place where they were needed. The person carrying them must herself be like a log: heavy and ungainly but full of strength and potential. 'Everything must find its place and one must try to understand what it can be used for... I carry more and more steadily now. I breathe in a new way, my sweat is salt.'

Now it was nearly dusk and still raining. Her repeated trek up and down the hill had come to seem unreal in a calm, automatic way, and as she trudged up and down again and again she entered a dizzy state of lifting and carrying and balancing, of throwing timber down against the wall and then going up again, and as she did this she became strong and sure of herself, which smoothed out all her words and clipped them short. Props, boards, planks, logs. She pulled off her sweaters and let them lie in the rain. 'The result of what I'm doing will be what I want. I'm moving what's in the wrong place so it will end up in the right place. My legs are tensing in my boots. I could carry rocks. Lever them and roll them with crowbar and pulley, enormous rocks, build a wall round myself in which each rock would have its own place. But maybe it's pointless to build a wall round an island.'

When it grew dark she felt tired. Her legs began shaking, she let the heavy logs lie and carried boards. In the end she was reduced to lining up small pieces of wood in rows against the wall of the house. And small, worrying thoughts came to her. Maybe the squirrel didn't just use the exterior of the woodpile as a shelter but lived right inside it where it was really dry. She'd done the wrong thing. Every time she'd moved a plank, that particular plank might have been the roof of the squirrel's home. Every time she lifted something, she might have been causing disturbance or destruction. Anyone altering the shape of the woodpile should have calculated carefully how the logs lay, how they balanced against one another, should have considered the matter calmly and judiciously, so as to know whether a deliberate sharp heave would have been best or a cautious bit of patient coaxing.

She listened to the whispering silence lying over the island, to the rain and the night. 'It's impossible,' she thought. 'I'll never go there again.' She went back to the cottage and undressed and lay down. This evening she didn't light the lamp, a breach of ritual, but it showed the squirrel how little she cared what happened on the island.

Next morning the squirrel didn't come to eat. She waited a long time but it didn't come. There was no reason why it should be offended or suspicious. Everything she'd done had been simple, unambiguous and just: she'd divided the woodpile between them and withdrawn. More than just, the squirrel's woodpile was many times bigger than hers. If the animal had the slightest personal confidence in her, if it was capable of understanding that she was a living creature and well disposed, then surely it must have grasped that from start to finish all she had done was try to help.

She sat down at the table, sharpened her pencil and set out the paper in front of her, at right angles and parallel with the edge of the table; this always helped her to understand the squirrel better.

So if now, despite everything, the squirrel saw her merely as something that moved, an object, something trivial and unimportant, then it might be equally unlikely to consider her an enemy. She tried to concentrate, she made a serious attempt to understand how the squirrel might perceive her and in what way the scare at the woodpile might have changed its attitude to her. Perhaps it had been on the point of forming an attachment to her only to be gripped by distrust at the crucial moment. If on the other hand it thought her of no importance, just a part of the island, a part of everything that was withering and marking autumn's progress towards winter, then, as we've seen, it would be unlikely to consider the episode at the woodpile an aggressive act, but more a sort of storm, a change that — She felt tired and began to draw squares and triangles on the paper, as she did so, understanding the squirrel less and less. She drew long twisting lines to connect the squares and triangles, and tiny leaves growing out in all directions. The rain had stopped. The sea was swollen and shiny; what endless nonsense people talked about the sea being beautiful. And then she saw the boat.

It was far off but moving, approaching, a black inorganic form that was neither gull nor stone nor navigation buoy. The boat was coming straight for the island, and there was nowhere else for it to come. Boats seen from the side are harmless, passing by in the shipping lanes, but this one was coming straight on, black as fly shit.

She clawed at her papers. Some fluttered to the floor: she tried to gather them up into the drawer but they crumpled and wouldn't go in, and anyway it was wrong, completely wrong, to hide them. They should stay in view, discouraging and protecting. She pulled them out again and smoothed them down. Who was this coming, daring to come? It was them, the others, now they'd found her. She ran about the room moving chairs and other objects and then moved them back again because the room must remain as it was. The black spot had come nearer. She grabbed the edge of the table with both hands, stood still and listened for the sound of a motor. There was no way round it, they were coming. They were coming, straight at her.

When the sound of the motor was very near, she threw open the window at the back of the cottage, jumped out and ran. It was too late to launch the boat. She crouched and ran onwards to the far side of the island, where she slid down into a crevice near the water. From here the motor was inaudible – you could only hear the slow movement of the sea against the rocks. 'What if they come ashore? They can see my boat here. If they find the cottage empty, they'll begin wondering, they'll go up into the island and find me. Crouching here. That won't do. It won't do at all, I must go back.' She began to crawl, more slowly, towards the crest of the island. The motor had been switched off; they'd landed. She lay full length in the wet grass, edged forward a few metres and raised herself on her elbows to look.

The boat had anchored in the shallows off the island, and the people in it were getting down to some fly-fishing. Three square men sitting with their lines and drinking coffee from a Thermos. They may have been talking a bit; now and then they pulled a line in; perhaps they were catching some fish. Her neck was tired and she let her head sink onto her arms. She didn't care about squirrels, or fly-fishermen, or anyone, but just let herself slip down into a great disappointment and admit she was disappointed. 'How can this be possible?' she thought frankly. 'How can I be so angry that they've come at all and then so dreadfully disappointed that they haven't landed?'

Next day she decided not to get out of bed, a melancholy and admirable decision. She thought no further than: 'I shall never get up again.' It was raining, with an even, calm rain that might continue indefinitely. 'Good, I like rain. Curtains and draperies and endless rain going on and on, pattering, rustling, spattering on the roof, not like the challenge of sunshine that moves hour by hour through the room, over the window-ledge and the carpet, marking afternoon on the rocking-chair and finally vanishing on the chimney breast, red as an indictment. Today's a respectable and straightforward grey day, an anonymous day outside time; it doesn't count.'

She made a warm hollow for her heavy body and pulled the quilt over her head. Through the little airhole left for her nose, she could see two pink roses on the wallpaper; nothing could reach her. Slowly she drifted into sleep again. She'd taught herself to spend more and more time asleep. She loved sleep.

The rainy weather was darkening into evening when she woke feeling hungry. It was very cold in the room. She pulled the quilt round her and went down into the cellar for a can of food. She'd forgotten her torch and picked up a can at random in the darkness, then stood listening, uneasy, can in hand. The squirrel was somewhere in the cellar. She heard a tiny scurrying sound, then silence. But she knew it was there. It would live in her cellar all winter and its nest might be anywhere. The hole must stay open, it mustn't be allowed to get snowed up again. All the cans of food, everything she needed, must be taken up into the house. And even so she'd never be sure whether the squirrel was living in the cellar or the woodpile.

She came up and closed the trapdoor after her. The can she was holding was meat with dill and she didn't like meat with dill. A belt of clear sky had opened on the horizon, a narrow glowing band of sunset. The islands lay like coal-black streaks and lumps on a blazing sea, burning right up to the shore where the swell was surging and gliding over and over again in the same curve round the promontory against the slippery November hill. She ate slowly and watched the red deepen over sky and sea, an unbelievably violent red, till it suddenly went out and everything was violet, shading slowly into grey and early night.

She was very much awake now. She dressed and lit the lamp and all the candles she could find, then lit the fire and laid her shining torch beside the window. Finally she hung the paper lantern outside the door, where it shone clear and still in the peaceful night. Then she took what was left of the Madeira and set the bottle on the table beside the glass. She went out onto the hill, leaving the door open. The shining house was beautiful and as full of secrets as an illuminated window on an unknown boat. She went further, right out to the end of the promontory and began to circle the island, very slowly, at the very edge of the water, constantly turning her face towards the wide-open darkness of the sea.

It was only when she'd gone round the whole island and come back to the promontory that she would allow herself to turn and look at her radiant house, and when she'd done that she would go straight back into the warmth, shut the door behind her and be at home. When she came into her house the squirrel was sitting on the table. It panicked and knocked over the bottle, which started rolling; she threw herself forward too late and the bottle fell and smashed on the floor, leaving broken glass between her fingers and the carpet quickly darkening with wine.

She raised her head and looked at the squirrel. It was sitting among her books as if fixed to the wall, its legs apart in a heraldic pose, motionless. She got up and took a step towards it, then another step; when it didn't move, she stretched out her hand and came nearer, very slowly,

and the squirrel bit her like lightning, sharp as slicing scis-
sors. She screamed and screamed with anger in the empty
room, then stumbled across the fragments of glass and out
onto the hill, where she stood and roared at the squirrel.
Never had anyone ever forfeited her trust or abused
an unspoken understanding with her to the extent the
squirrel had. She wasn't sure whether she'd reached
out her hand to the animal to stroke it or to throttle
it. It made no difference – she had simply reached out
her hand. She went in and swept up the broken glass,
extinguished all the lights and built up the fire. Then she
burned everything she'd written about the squirrel.

In the time that followed, their rituals didn't change.
She put out food on the hill and the squirrel came and
ate. She didn't know where it was living and didn't want
to know; to show her contempt, an indifference that
didn't condescend to revenge, she no longer went near
the cellar or the woodpile on the hill. But, this apart,
she moved violently about the island, rushing out of the
cottage and slamming the door after her, clattering and
stamping, and in the end she took to running. She would
stand still a very long time, entirely motionless, before
setting off over the hill, backwards and forwards across
the island, puffing and blowing as she ran, waving her
arms and screaming. She didn't give a damn whether the
squirrel saw her or not.

One morning she woke to find it had been snowing,
a thick covering of unmelting snow. Now the frost had

come she must go in to town, buy things, get the motor
going. She went and looked at the motor, lifted it up for
a while, then put it back against the cottage wall. Maybe
after a few days, there was a strong wind. Instead she
started looking for the squirrel's footprints in the snow.
The ground was white and unmarked near the cellar and
the woodpile; she went round the shore and systemati-
cally over the whole island, but found no tracks but her
own, clear and black, cutting the island into squares and
triangles and long curves. Later in the day she became
suspicious and searched under the furniture in the cottage,
opened cupboards and drawers, and even climbed up onto
the roof and looked down the chimney. "You're making a
fool of me, you devil," she told the squirrel.

Then she went out to the promontory to count the
pieces of board, the squirrel-boats she'd set out ready
for a favourable wind to the mainland just to show the
squirrel how little she cared what it did or where it went.
They were still there, all six of them. But for a moment
she was unsure: had there been six or seven? She should
have written down the number. How could she not have
written it down. She went back to the cottage, shook out
the carpet and swept. These days everything was happening in the wrong order. Sometimes she cleaned her teeth
in the evening and didn't bother to light the lamp. All
because she no longer had any Madeira left to help divide
the day into proper periods, defining them and making
them easier to remember.

She cleaned the windows and reorganised her book-
shelves, this time not by writers but alphabetically.

When she'd done this, she thought of a better and more personal system: she would have the books she liked best on the top shelf and the ones she liked least on the bottom. But she was astonished to find there wasn't a single book she really liked. So she left them as they were and sat by the window to wait for more snow. There was a bank of clouds to the south that looked promising.

That evening she felt a sudden need for company and went up on the hill with her walkie-talkie. She pulled out the aerial, switched on and listened: she heard a remote scratching and sighing. Once or twice she'd found herself in the middle of a conversation between two ships; perhaps that's what was happening now. She waited a long time. The night was pitch-black and very quiet; she closed her eyes, waiting patiently. Then she heard something, incredibly far away – no clear words, but two voices talking. Slow and calm, coming nearer, but she couldn't make out what they were saying. Then their tone changed and their speeches got shorter; it was clear they were bringing their conversation to an end and they said goodbye. She was too late.

She began screaming: "Hello, it's me, can you hear me?", though she knew they couldn't hear her, and then there was nothing left in the apparatus but the far-off sighing and she switched it off. "Stupid," she told herself. Then it occurred to her that the batteries she had might fit the radio and she went down to check. They were too small. She had to go to town. *Madeira, batteries.* Under batteries she wrote *nuts* and crossed it out again. The squirrel had gone – there was no doubt there had been seven pieces of board, not six, all at exactly the same distance from the water: sixty-five centimetres. She read through her list and suddenly it looked like an inventory in a foreign language, nothing whatever to do with her: *sheer-pins, embrocation, dried milk, batteries* – a list of unreal and hostile objects. The only thing that mattered was the boards: had there been six or seven? She took her measuring-rod and torch and went out again. The shore was empty, absolutely clean. There were no pieces of board there any more, not a single one; the sea had risen and taken them away.

She couldn't believe her eyes. She stood at the water's edge, shining her torch down into the sea. The light broke the surface, illuminating a grey-green underwater grotto full of small indefinite particles she'd never noticed before; the grotto grew progressively dimmer the deeper it went. She lifted the torch and shone it out over the water into the darkness. The weak cone of light was captured by a colour out there, a clear yellow, a varnished boat being driven away from land by the wind.

She didn't immediately understand that it was her own boat; she just watched it, noticing for the first time how helpless and dramatic the movements of an empty, drifting boat are. But the boat wasn't empty. The squirrel was sitting in the stern, staring blindly straight into the light like a cardboard shape, a dead toy.

She made half a movement towards taking off her boots, but stopped. The torch was lying on the rock, shining obliquely down into the water, revealing a bank of swollen seagrass disturbed by the rising sea, then darkness where the hill curved downwards. It was too far out, too cold. Too late. She took a careless step and the torch slid down into the water. It didn't go out at once, but continued shining as it sank down along the slope of the hill, gradually fading amid brief glimpses of ghostly brown landscapes and moving shadows, then nothing but darkness.

"You damn squirrel," she said softly, in admiration. She stayed on standing in the darkness, still amazed, a little weak in the legs and not quite sure whether or not everything had now utterly changed.

It took a long time to make her way back gradually across the island. It wasn't until she'd shut the door behind her that she felt relieved, hugely exhilarated. Every decision had been taken away from her. She no longer had a need to hate the squirrel or concern herself about it in any way. She had no need to write about it, no need to write anything at all. Everything had been decided and resolved with clear and absolute simplicity.

Outside it had begun to snow, heavily and peacefully – winter had come. She put more wood on the fire and turned up the lamp. She went to the kitchen table and began to write, very fast. One windless day in November, near sunrise, she saw a human being at the landing place...

Letters from Klara

Dear Matilda,

You're hurt because I forgot your venerable birthday. That's unreasonable of you. I know the only reason you've looked forward to getting birthday greetings from me all these years is because I'm three years younger than you are. But it's time you realised that the passing of the years isn't in itself a feather in your cap.

You're asking for Guidance from Above, excellent. But while you're waiting for it to arrive, might it not be profitable to discuss a few bad habits which I have to admit aren't totally alien to me, either.

My dear Matilda, one thing we should all remember is not to grumble if we can possibly help it, because grumbling immediately gives bad habits the upper hand.

I know you've been fortunate enough to enjoy astonishingly good health, but you do have a unique capacity for giving those round you a bad conscience by grumbling, and then of course they hit back by cheerfully writing you off as someone who no longer matters. I know, I've seen it. Whatever it is you want or don't want, couldn't you stop whining? Why not try raising your voice instead and shaking them up with a few strong words or, best of all, scaring them a bit? I know very well you're capable of it: there was never any mewing in the old days, far from it.

And all that stuff about not being able to get to sleep at night, presumably because you catnap eight times a day. Yes, I know; it's true that memory has an unfortunate habit of working backwards at night and gnawing its way through everything without sparing the slightest detail – that you were too much of a coward to do something, for instance; that you made a wrong choice, or were tactless or unfeeling or criminally unobservant – but of course no one but you has given a thought for years to these things which to you are calamities, shameful actions and irretrievably stupid statements! Isn't it unfair, when we're endowed with such sharp memories, that they only function in reverse?

Dear Matilda, do write and tell me what you think about these sensitive matters. I promise I'll try not to be a know-all; oh yes, don't deny it, you have called me that in the past. But I'd be fascinated to know, for example, what you do when you can't remember how many times you've said the same thing to the same person. Do you extricate yourself by starting off 'So, as I said...' or 'As I may have already said...'? Or what?... Have you any other suggestions? Or d'you just keep quiet?

And do you let conversations you can't follow continue over your head? Do you ever try to make a sensible contribution only to find that everyone else has moved on to a completely different subject? Do you try to save face by telling them they're talking nonsense or wasting their time on matters too trivial to be worth discussing? In general, are we any of us in the least interested? Please reassure me that we are!

Only if you write to me, please don't use that antediluvian fountain pen of yours; it makes your writing illegible, and in any case it's hopelessly out of date. Get them to buy you some felt pens, medium point 0.5mm. You can get them anywhere.

Yours,
Klara

PS I read somewhere that anything written in felt pen becomes illegible after about forty years. How about that? Good, don't you think? Or are you planning to write your memoirs? You know the sort of thing: 'Not to be read for fifty years' (I hope you think that's funny).

Dear Ewald,

What a nice surprise to get a letter from you. What gave you the idea of writing?

Yes, of course we can meet; it's been ages, as you say. Something like sixty years, I think.

And thank you for all the nice things you wrote – maybe a little too nice, my dear old friend. Hasn't time made you a little sentimental?

Yes, I think growing roses is a great idea! I understand there's a very practical gardening programme on the radio every Saturday morning, repeated on Sundays. Why not listen to it?

Give me a call any time, but remember it may take me a while to get to the phone. And don't forget to say whether you're still a vegetarian, because I want to make us a really special dinner.

Yes, do bring your photograph album, I hope we'll be able to have a reasonable stab at dealing with the inevitable 'd'you remembers', and then go on to talk about whatever comes into our heads.

Yours sincerely,
Klara

Hi Steffy!

Thanks for the bark boat, it's beautiful and it's lovely to have it. I tried it out in the bath and it balances perfectly.

Don't worry about that report, tell Daddy and Mummy it's sometimes much more important to be able to work with your hands and make something beautiful.

I'm sorry about the cat. But if she lived to be seventeen she was probably quite tired and no longer very well. The words you wrote for her grave aren't bad but you must take care with the rhythm. We'll talk more about that when we meet.

Your godmother,
Klara

Dear Mr Öhlander,

In your letter of the 27th you claim that I am unjustifiably withholding from you an early work of your own, which you say you need to have, as soon as possible, for a retrospective exhibition.

I cannot remember that during a visit to your niece's son I 'wangled' the picture in question out of him; he is much more likely to have pressed me to remove it from his flat.

I have made a careful study of the signatures on the works I have round me here and can just about make out one which could possibly be your own. The picture seems to show something halfway between an interior and a landscape; one might say that there's a *je ne sais quoi* of the semi-abstract about it.

The size, which you didn't mention, is the classic French 50 x 61.

I'm restoring your work to you by return of post and I hope that it will now be able to take its rightful place in your collection.

Yours faithfully,
Klara Nygård

Dear Nicholas,

I expect you've only just got back from your 'mystery destination' (I have a strong feeling it was Majorca); be that as it may, I've decided to make yet another small change to my will. Don't groan, I know that deep down all this toing and froing amuses you.

Well, I want to make over a fixed annual sum to the Old People's Home of whose services I shall one day be availing myself. But – and this is the important point – only during my lifetime. Interest from banks and bonds and whatever else, I can do without – you know more about that than I do. They can use the money in whatever way suits them best.

I'm sure you've got the idea, cunning as you are. This temporary extra income will make it worth their while, at the Home, to do their best to keep me alive as long as they can; I shall be their mascot and will obviously be able to take certain liberties. What's left when I die will not go to them but must be divided up exactly as we planned earlier.

By the way, I'm in excellent health and I hope you are too.

Klara

My dear Cecilia,

It was so nice of you to send me my old letters; what an enormous box, did you at least have someone to help you get it to the post? It really touches me that you saved them all (and even numbered them), but, my dear, that business of reading them through – you understand what I mean? I suppose the stamps were cut off for some stamp-collecting child. But if you have any other correspondence from the beginning of the century you should keep the whole envelope, stamps and all; that'll make the stamps much more desirable to a philatelist – and be specially careful with blocks of four.

I assume you're busy clearing out the house – very natural. Congratulations! I'm doing the same and I've been gradually learning all kinds of things, one being that if you give special treasures to young people they're not usually particularly pleased to have them. If you persist, they get more and more polite and more and more irritated. Have you noticed? But, do you know, there's a flea market every Saturday and Sunday in Sandvikstorg square these days – how about that? Anyone can go there and find what they want for themselves without needing to feel either put upon or grateful. Brilliant idea.

You say you're gloomy and depressed but that's normal, Cecilia, nothing to worry about. I've read somewhere that it's a physiological phenomenon, doesn't that make you feel better? I mean, you feel depressed, so you sit down and think, 'Oh well, it doesn't matter, there's nothing I can do about it, it's just the way things are.' Isn't that the truth?

What else shall I tell you – oh, yes, I've got rid of my pot plants and I'm trying to learn a little French. You know, I've always admired you; you speak the language so perfectly. What's that elegant way they have of ending a letter? – *Chère madame*, I enclose you, no, me, in your – oh you know.

I'm just a beginner.

Chère petite madame, I do miss you sometimes –

Love,
Klara

Dear Sven Roger,

So good of you to make sure the porcelain tiled stove's in working order again. If those officials come back and say it's against the law to light it I shall speak to my solicitor; the stove's an article of Historic Importance, as we're all well aware.

When you come back from your holiday you'll find that Mrs Fagerholm from the floor above me has gone in for an unnecessarily sweeping clearance of her attic storage space. She parked her unnameable possessions in front of my own space, so I naturally threw the whole lot out into the corridor.

I remember you once said you'd like some indoor plants for your summer cottage. I've put my own collection of pot plants out in the yard next the wheelie bins and anyone's welcome to take what they want; anything left can go into the bins. I'll keep them watered for the time being. To explain my apparently heartless behaviour, I'd just like to say that these potted plants have weighed on my conscience for far too long; they always get either too little water or too much, one can never get it right.

By the way, don't hurry to wash the windows; they have what looks like an attractive light mist on them just at the moment; it would be a pity to disturb it. With my very best wishes for your summer holiday,

K. Nygård

PS Don't say anything to the Fagerholm woman. I have to admit I really enjoyed throwing out her rubbish.

Camilla Alleén
'Woman to Woman'

Dear Ms Alleén,

Thank you for your kind letter. But I do not consider myself to be in a position to take part, as you put it, in an enquiry into the problems and pleasures of old age.

One could of course maintain that, though taking part might be difficult, it could also be interesting – but I don't see any point in listing one's obvious misfortunes, while trying to describe what's interesting about being old seems to me to be a private matter most unsuited to the dogmatic statements demanded by questionnaires.

My dear Ms Alleén, I'm afraid you're not very likely to get many honest answers to your questions.

Yours sincerely,
Klara Nygård

Messages

I'll make it to Maritim, got hod of Gustafsson, van coming at 8, have redirected mail to summer address, bye kiss Tooti   Take last things out of fridge

Hi my name is Olavi. You write well but last time you didn't make a happy ending. Why do you do this?

We look forward to your valued reply soonest concerning Moomin motifs on toilet paper in pastel shades

Don't say too much if they ring, don't promise yet. Bye Tooti

Hi! We're three girls in a mad rush with our essays about you could you help us by saying in just a few words how you started writing and why and what life means to you and then a message to young people you know the kind of thing. Thanks in advance

Dear Miss Jansson, You must understand that the only way I can earn a living are panholders with Moomin figures which I design myself and make in the kitchen without any paid help at present. How would 6% be for a start

Hi, I'm thinking of becoming a writer, can you help me with a little information? Is it all right to send your MS to several publishers simultaneously and is it better or worse with illustrations? And about contracts

One shimmering moonlit night I got up and do you know what I did ... I went out into the park and danced in my nightie! Maybe no one saw me but maybe someone ... Do you understand? Write

You are a really sinful person on top of everything else, but don't think you're safe, you're being watched every moment because we're there and we're waiting

My dear friend, I've been thinking of you so long now that it's really time I plucked up courage to ask a little boon of you; could you sometime when you feel like it draw all your sweet little figures in colour for my granddaughter Emanuela

Hi coming later heat the soup
Kiss, T

My hamsters have been named after you and your brother. I had a christening party on my fortieth birthday but Astrid Lindgren didn't come.

You each had a rosette round your tummy. It's been an uncommonly cold winter and folk who are uncared for freeze to death, one morning you were both dead on the balcony. I'm thinking of having a funeral on Riddarholmen island, best wishes

We are contacting you in connection with this year's marmalade promotion, in the first instance wondering if there would be any chance of a previously unpublished Moomin comic strip on the theme of marmalade

What steel pen do you use to draw your comic strips? Everything I've found seems old-fashioned and the new ones are useless. Can you give me a copy of the usual contract and I'd also very much like to know a little more about world rights

Dear Miss Jansson
I have produced Moomin pictures for my home and also for profit and pleasure and placed them for sale in art galleries and kiosks bordering busy traffic routes. Now one of my friends is saying one ought to ask permission, can this be true? If I don't hear from you before week 5 shall go on as usual

Insufficient address
Father Christmas Moomin Valley.
Please give current address and surname

We are fully aware that you had planned a black troll for our Moomin liquorice advertisement, but for technical reasons

What shall I do with my parents, they're becoming more and more hopeless. Write!

Couldn't we meet and chat about the old days at school? I'm Margit, the one who punched you in the stomach in the playground

We look forward to your comments concerning the fore-going account in connection with earlier uncompleted agreements and taking into account secondary effects to which our most recent market discharge may have given rise we would be glad if in urgent order

Now don't be afraid, but have you any understand-ing whatever of what your comic strips can mean for expectant mothers, how great a responsibility you bear? Have you even remotely grasped what it can mean for expectant mothers to be constantly confronted with those snouts – how do you think the next generation may look

My cat's died! Write at once

Hi dear unknown fairy-tale auntie, we're a group of young folks with Ideas! What d'you think? Are you up for it?
Luv, Plastic Ltd, 'Now or Never' project

Dear Jansson san
I have collected money for a long time. I will come and sit at your feet to understand. Please when can I come there?

Last night they came in again. They're everywhere. Please come, I implore you

Could you consider becoming patron of this constantly threatened little area of natural beauty

How could you even consider invading this constantly threatened little area of natural beauty

We've launched a discreet new mini sanitary towel – earlier design Peach Bloom Ltd – but now we're aiming at a younger clientele with the slogan 'Hi there, Little My always plays safe' – a bit of fun which with your kind permission

Can't you draw me a Snufkin that I can have tattooed on my arm as a symbol of freedom

I don't know why I'm writing but I must because my heart is so big tonight throw away these lines forget them don't bother to read them if you feel embarrassed but please be terribly kind and answer if you possibly can

It was you who murdered Karin Boye*

Hi, took the mail with me
Kiss, T

Is it OK for you to transfer my fee to Sri Lanka? My latest translation into Esperanto can't be ready till New Year. I hope you will be patient

In your story The Cat you change cat twice and that's heartless. As a member of the RSPCA I must

I thought it might make you happy to know that there is someone who has everything that life can offer. It's true of me and I'm thankful. But the one thing I long to do is create. My therapist recommends watercolours and suggested I should phone you. It's a matter of choice of colours and motifs

My very dear friend you are wallowing in sin. A Voice has spoken to me and now I pray for you every night which makes me so tired. I enclose some Tracts, read them and let me know if things go better. Hold out. There is an explanation and forgiveness for everything

* Karin Boye: Swedish poet, novelist and story writer who took her own life in 1941.

This is a message in a bottle for Toffle from Australia. If the paper gets wet on the way ask your mummy to iron it dry

Have you forgotten your baby's fiftieth birthday? Have you read my letters? Have you got my presents? Don't tell me you're old and tired. I won't stop writing – I'll never let go of you!

I brought the washing in, you can put the potatoes on at 6. Someone called Anttiia phoned

Dear Jansson san
Take good care of yourself in this dangerous world
Please have a long life
With love

Correspondence

Dear Jansson san

I'm a girl from Japan.
I'm thirteen years old and two months.
On the eighth of January I'll be fourteen.
I have a mother and two little sisters.
I've read everything you've written.
When I've read something I read it one more time.
Then I think about snow and how to be alone.
Tokyo's a very big city.
I'm learning English and studying very seriously.
I love you.
I dream one day I'll be as old as you and as clever as you.
I have many dreams.
There's a Japanese kind of poem called haiku.

I'm sending you a haiku in Japanese
It's about cherry flowers.
Do you live in a big forest?

Forgive me for writing to you.
I wish you good health and a long life.
Tamiko Atsumi

Dear Jansson san

My new birthday today is very important.
Your present is very important to me.
Everyone admires your present and the picture of the
little island where you live.
It's hanging above my bed.
How many lonely islands are there in Finland?
Can anyone live there who wants to?
I want to live on an island.
I love lonely islands and I love flowers and snow.
But I can't write how they are.
I'm studying very seriously.
I read your books in English.
Your books aren't the same in Japanese.
Why are they different?
I think you are happy.
Look after your health very carefully.

I wish you a long life.
Tamiko Atsumi

Dear Jansson san

It's been a long time, for five months and nine days
    you haven't written to me.
Did you get my letters?
Did you get the presents?
I long for you.
You must understand that I'm studying very seriously.
Now I'll tell you about my dream.
My dream is to travel to other countries and learn their
    languages and learn to understand.
I want to be able to talk with you.
I want you to talk with me.
You must tell me how you describe things without
    seeing other houses and with no one getting in the way.
I want to know how to write about snow.
I want to sit at your feet and learn.
I'm collecting money so I can travel.
Now I'm sending you a new haiku.
It's about a very old woman who sees blue mountains
    far away.
When she was young she didn't see them.
Now she can't reach them.
That's a beautiful haiku.

I beg you please be careful.
    Tamiko

Dear Jansson san

You were going to go on a great long journey, now
　you've been travelling more than six months.
I think you've come back again.
Where did you go, my Jansson san, and what did you
　learn on your journey?
Perhaps you took with you a kimono.
In autumn colours and autumn is the time to travel.
But you've said so often that time is short.
My time grows long when I think of you.
I want to become old like you and have only big
　clever thoughts.
I keep your letters in a very beautiful box in a
　secret place.
I read them again at sundown.

　Tamiko

Dear Jansson san

Once you wrote to me when it was summer in Finland
　and you were living on the lonely island.
You've told me that post hardly ever comes to your
　island.
Then do you get many letters from me at once?
You say it feels nice when the ships go by and
　don't stop.

But now it's winter in Finland.
You've written a book about winter, you've
    described my dream.
I'll write a story to help everyone understand and
    recognise their own dream.
How old must you be to write a story?
But I can't write my story without you.
Every day is a day of waiting.
You've said you're so tired.
You work and there are too many people.
But I want to be the one who comforts you and
    protects your solitude.
This is a sad haiku about someone who waited too
    long for the one they loved.
You see how it went!
But it's not so good in translation.
Has my English got any better?

Always
    Tamiko

Much loved Jansson san, thank you!

Yes, that's how it is, you don't have to be a certain
age, you just begin writing a story because you have
to, about what you know or also about what you long

for, about your dream, the unknown. O much loved
Jansson san. One mustn't worry about others and
what they think and understand, because while you're
telling a story you're only concerned with the story
and yourself. Then you really are on your own. At
this moment I know all about what it's like to love
someone far away and I will hurry to write about it
before she comes nearer. I send you a haiku again, it's
about a little stream which becomes happy in spring so
everyone listens and feels delight. I can't translate it.
Listen to me Jansson san and write to say when I can
come. I've collected money and I think I'll get a travel
scholarship. What month would be best and most
beautiful for our meeting?

Tamiko

Dear Jansson san

Thank you for your very wise letter.
I understand the forest's big in Finland and the sea
    too but your house is very small.
It's a beautiful thought, to meet a writer only in
    her books.
I'm learning all the time.

I wish you good health and a long life.
    Your Tamiko Atsumi

My Jansson san

It's been snowing all day.
I'm learning to write about snow.
Today my mother died.
When you're the eldest in your family in Japan, you
    can't leave home and don't want to.
I hope you understand me.
I thank you.
The poem is by Lang Shih Yiian, who was once a
    great poet in China.
It has been translated into your language by Hwang
    Tsu-Yii and Alf Henrikson.
"Wild geese scream shrilly on muffled winds.
The morning snow is heavy, weather cloudy and cold.
Poor, I can give you nothing in parting
but the blue mountains and they'll always be with you."

Tamiko

Travelling Light

I WISH I COULD DESCRIBE THE ENORMOUS RELIEF I FELT when they finally pulled up the gangway! Only then did I feel safe. Or, more exactly, when the ship had moved far enough from the quay for it to be impossible for anyone to call out... ask for my address, scream that something awful had happened... Believe me, you can't imagine my giddy sense of freedom. I unbuttoned my overcoat and took out my pipe but my hands were shaking and I couldn't light it; but I stuck it between my teeth anyway, because that somehow establishes a certain detachment from one's surroundings. I went as far forward as possible in the bows, from where it was impossible to see the city, and hung over the railing like the most carefree traveller you can imagine. The sky was light blue, the little clouds seemed whimsical, pleasantly capricious...

Everything was in the past now, gone, of no significance; nothing mattered any more, no one was important. No telephone, no letters, no doorbell. Of course you have no idea what I'm referring to, but it doesn't matter anyway; in fact I shall merely assert that everything had been sorted out to the best of my ability, thoroughly taken care of down to the smallest detail. I wrote the letters I had to write – in fact I'd done that as long ago as the day before, announcing my sudden departure without explanation and without in any way accounting for my behaviour. It was very difficult; it took a whole day. Naturally I left no information about where I was going and indicated no time for my return, since I have no intention of ever coming back. The caretaker's wife will look after my houseplants; those tired living things – which never look well no matter how much trouble one takes over them – have made me feel very uneasy. Never mind: I shan't ever have to see them again.

Perhaps it might interest you to know what I packed? As little as possible! I've always dreamed of travelling light, a small weekend bag of the sort one can casually whisk along with oneself as one walks with rapid but unhurried steps through, shall we say, the departure lounge of an airport, passing a mass of nervous people dragging along large heavy cases. This was the first time I'd succeeded in taking the absolute minimum with me, ruthless in the face of family treasures and those little objects one can become so attached to that remind one of... well, of emotional bits of one's life – no, that least of all! My bag was as light as my happy-go-lucky heart and contained nothing more than one would need for a routine night at a hotel. I left the flat without leaving instructions of any kind, but I did clean it, very thoroughly. I'm very good at cleaning. Then I turned off the electricity, opened the fridge and unplugged the phone. That was the very last thing, the definitive step; now I'd done with them.

And during all this time the phone never rang once – a good omen. Not one, not a single one of all these, these – but I don't want to talk about them now, I'm not going to worry about them any more, no, they no longer occupy even a single second of my thoughts. Well, when I'd pulled out the phone plug and checked one last time that I had all the papers I needed in my pocket-book – passport, tickets, travellers' cheques, pension card – I looked out of the window to make sure that there were some taxis waiting at the stand on the corner, shut the front door and let the keys fall through the letterbox.

Out of old habit I avoided the lift; I don't like lifts. On the second floor I tripped and grabbed hold of the banisters, and stood still a moment, suddenly hot all over. Think, just think – what if I'd really fallen, perhaps sprained my ankle or worse? Everything would have been in vain, fatal, irreparable. It would have been unthinkable to get ready and gather myself together to leave a second time. In the taxi I felt so exhilarated I carried on a lively conversation with the driver, commenting on the early spring weather and taking an interest in this and that relating to his profession, but he hardly responded at all. I pulled myself together, because this was exactly what I'd decided to avoid; from now on I was going to be a person who never took any interest in anyone. The problems that might face a taxi driver were nothing to do with me. We reached the boat much too early, he lifted out my bag, I thanked him and gave him too big a tip. He didn't smile, which upset me a bit, but the man who took my ticket was very friendly.

My journey had started. It gradually got cold on deck, there was hardly anyone else there and I presumed the other passengers must have made their way to the restaurant. Taking my time, I went to find my cabin. I saw at once that I wasn't going to be alone; someone had left a coat, pocket-book and umbrella on one of the bunks, and two elegant suitcases were standing in the middle of the floor. Discreetly, I moved them out of the way. Naturally I had demanded, or more accurately expressed a desire to have, a cabin to myself; sleeping on my own has become very important to me and on this journey in particular it was absolutely essential for me to, so to speak, savour my new independence entirely undisturbed. I couldn't possibly go and complain to the purser, who would have merely pointed out that the boat was full, that it was a regrettable misunderstanding, and that if the misunderstanding were to be rectified I would be aware all night as I lay on my solitary bunk that the man who was to have shared my cabin was having to spend the night sleepless on a deckchair.

I noticed that his toilet articles were of exclusive quality, and I was particularly impressed by his light-blue electric toothbrush and a miniature case with the monogram A.C. on it. I unpacked my own toothbrush and the other things I had considered necessary from my ascetic point of view, laid out my pyjamas on the other bunk and asked myself if I was hungry. The thought of the likely crush in the restaurant put me off, so I decided to skip dinner and have a drink in the bar instead. The bar was pretty empty this early in the evening. I sat down on one of the high stools, propped my feet on the traditional metal railing which runs round every bar on the continent, and lit my pipe.

"A Black and White if you please," I said to the bartender, accepting the glass with a brief nod and making clear with my attitude that I had no inclination for conversation. I sat and pondered the Idea of Travel; that is to say, the act of travelling unfettered and with no responsibility for what one has left behind and without any opportunity to foresee what may lie ahead and prepare for it. Nothing but an enormous sense of peace. It occurred to me to think back over my earlier journeys, every one of them, and I realised to my astonishment that this must be the first time I had ever travelled alone. First came my trips with my mother – Majorca and the Canaries. Majorca again. After mother went away I travelled with Cousin Herman, to Lübeck and Hamburg. He was only interested in museums, though they depressed him; he'd never been able to study painting and he couldn't get over it. Not a happy trip. Then the Wahlströms, who didn't know whether to divorce or not and thought it would be easier to travel as a threesome.

Where did we go..? Oh, yes of course, Venice. And during the mornings they quarrelled. No, that wasn't much of a journey. What next? A trip with a party to Leningrad. It was damn cold... And then Aunt Hilda who needed a break but didn't dare go by herself... but that was only as far as Mariehamn; we went to the Maritime Museum there, I remember. You see, when I went through all my life's journeys in my thoughts, any fear I possibly could have had that the way I'd decided to do things might not be right disappeared. I turned to the bartender, said, "Another, if you please," and looked round the bar, very much at ease. People had started coming in; happy well-fed people who ordered coffee and drinks to their tables and crowded round me at the bar.

Normally I very much dislike crowds and do everything I can to avoid being involved with them, even in buses and trams, but that evening it felt pleasant and sociable to be one among many, almost secure. An elderly gentleman with a cigar intimated with a discreet gesture that he needed my ashtray; "Of course, don't mention it," I responded and was on the point of begging his pardon but remembered in time: I'd finished with all that kind of thing. In an entirely matter-of-fact way, if with a certain nonchalance, I moved the ashtray to his side and calmly studied myself in the mirror behind the bottles in the bar.

There's something special about a bar, don't you think? A place for chance happenings, for possibilities to become reality, a refuge on the awkward route from should to must. But, I must confess, not the sort of place I've much frequented. Now, as I sat and looked in the mirror, my face suddenly seemed rather agreeable. I suppose I had never allowed myself time to look closely at the appearance time has given me. A thin face with somewhat surprised but frankly beautiful eyes, hair admittedly grey but luxuriant in an almost artistic manner, with a lock hanging down over my brow giving me an expression of – what shall we say – anxious watchfulness? Watchful concern? No. Just watchfulness. I emptied my glass and suddenly felt an urgent need to communicate, but held it in check. At all events, despite everything, wasn't this precisely an occasion when, at last, I would not be forced to listen but could be allowed to talk myself, freely and recklessly? Among men, in a bar? For example, entirely in passing of course, I might let slip information about my decisive contribution at the Post Office. But no. Absolutely not. Be secretive – don't make confidences; at most, drop hints...

Sitting on my left was a young man who seemed extremely restless. He kept moving his position, turning this way and that on his stool and seemingly trying to keep an eye on everything that was happening in the room. I turned to the neighbour on my other side and said: "Very crowded this evening. Looks like we're in for a calm crossing." He stubbed his cigar in the ashtray and remarked that the boat was full and that our wind speed was eight metres per second, though they'd forecast it would get stronger during the night. I liked his calm matter-of-fact manner and asked myself whether he was retired and why he should be on his way to London.

Let me tell you, my interest surprised myself; nothing has become so utterly foreign, almost hateful to me, to be avoided at all costs, as curiosity and sympathy, any disposition to encourage in the slightest degree the surrounding world's irresistible need to start talking about its troubles. This is something I really do know about; during a long life I've heard most things and I've brought this entirely on myself. But, as I've said, I was sitting in a bar on the way to my new freedom – and I was being a bit careless.

He said: "You're going to London? On business?"

"No. Sea travel amuses me."

He nodded in appreciation. I could see his face in the mirror, a rather heavy face somewhat the worse for wear with a drooping moustache and tired eyes. He seemed elegant, expensively dressed, in a continental style, if you understand what I mean.

"When I was young," he said, "I worked out that it should be possible to travel by sea all the time, without stopping, meals included, for very much less than it costs to live in a city."

I watched him, fascinated, waiting for him to go on, but he said nothing more. Thank goodness, this was clearly not a man to make personal confidences. Meanwhile, soft music was throbbing persistently some-where up in the ceiling and people had begun talking with increasing animation, while trays heavily laden with glasses were being carried with impressive speed and precision between the tables. I thought: 'Here I am sitting with an experienced traveller, a man who has

taken the best from life and knows what he's talking about.' It was then he took out his pocket-book and showed me pictures of his family and his dog. That was a warning signal. A sharp sense of disappointment pierced me – but why should I be surprised if my companion was showing signs of behaving exactly like all the others? But I'd decided not to let anything whatever upset me, so I looked at his snapshots and said all the usual nice things. His wife, children, grandchildren and dog looked more or less just as one would expect, except that they seemed in an unusually flourishing condition.

He sighed – of course, I couldn't hear him sigh in all that din but I saw his broad shoulders rise and fall. Clearly not all was as it should be at home. I know; it's the same with them all. Even this most elegant, cigar-smoking traveller with his gold lighter and his family posing in front of his swimming pool – even him! I hurriedly began talking about the first thing that came into my head, the advantages of travelling light, and made up my mind to detach myself gradually from the man; I mean, get away as quickly as possible without seeming brusque. I dropped a hint by taking out my cabin key, laying it beside my glass and trying to catch the bartender's attention, naturally without success – the crush round the bar was worse than ever, increasingly impatient and loud, and the poor man was working like a maniac.

"Two Black and Whites," said my travel companion in a low voice but with the sort of calm, powerful authority that ensures immediate results. He fixed his heavy gaze on me and raised his glass. Now I was caught.

"Thanks," I said. "How nice – a little nightcap. It's getting rather late, I think."

He answered, "Not at all, Mr Melander. My name's Connaugh." And he laid his cabin key beside mine. "An incredible coincidence," I exclaimed, most put out.

"Oh no. I saw you coming out of the cabin. Your bag's very neatly labelled."

Suddenly I was jostled by the young man on my left as he leaned aggressively forward across the bar to demand a Cuba libre. He'd now had to ask three times but, no, everyone else must come first, typical, just what you'd expect... Mr Connaugh gave the youngster a very brief and very cold glance and said: "It seems to be time to get out of this place." But any relief I felt was destroyed by his next words: "I've got some whisky in the cabin and the night is long."

What could I do? Say I needed something to eat? He would have merely waited for me in the cabin. Now I could see him clearly: a forceful, dominating man who radiated unshakeable determination. Naturally I wanted to share the bill, but he dismissed the matter with a gesture and moved towards the door. I followed. We got into a crowded lift. The boat was teeming with people flocking round the fruit machines and sitting on the stairs. Their children were running all over the place and I was overcome by my old fear of crowds; when we finally reached the cabin I was trembling from head to foot. Mr Connaugh moved his luggage aside and took out a bottle of whisky, which he placed on the little table under the window; he had two silver cups as well. When he sat down the bunk creaked; it seemed altogether too puny and fragile for him. The cabin was first class, a bit of self-indulgence I'd allowed myself for this trip but which should have been reserved for me alone. It had a minibar, an elegant little arrangement which contained soft drinks, crisps and salted nuts. I opened its door.

"No," said Mr Connaugh, "not mineral water. Drink your whisky with plain water like the Scots. My father came from Scotland." I hurried to the bathroom and filled my toothmug, stumbling a little in the doorway, which had an unusually high threshold. "Ice?" I asked.

He shook his head. When he'd poured a little water into his whisky, he leaned back and drank. My voyage had suddenly been altered and my peace destroyed. I was sure he wouldn't go to bed for hours. "To you," he said. Everything repeats itself. "To you," I said.

"Journeys, journeys, to and fro. And you know exactly where you're going, every time. Home and away again, away and home again." "Not necessarily," I objected. "There are times..." but he interrupted me.

I'd thought of telling him that, so far as I was concerned, I hadn't booked any hotel and had no idea where I was going to end up. I wanted to give him a fairly adventurous picture of my new, virtually self-centred freedom but he'd already launched into an account of his worries: wife, children, grandchildren, house and dog, the last-named having clearly died in very distressing circumstances. I closed up completely. Perhaps for the first time in my life, I effectively managed to shut off that dreadful compassion which has given both myself and those round me such fearful trouble, I use that word deliberately: fearful. Now perhaps you can understand why I started on my journey? Perhaps you have some idea of the depth of my fatigue, of my exhaustion and nausea in the face of this constant need to feel sorry for people?

Of course, one can't help feeling sorry for people. Every single one of us is afflicted by some secret, insur-mountable disappointment, some form of anxiety or shame, and they sniff me out in no time. I mean, they know, their sense of smell leads them to me... Well, that's why I cleared off.

As I half-listened to Mr Connaugh I felt an enormous, and for me unaccustomed, anger gradually creeping over me. I emptied my glass and brutally interrupted him by saying, "Well, what d'you expect? Clearly you've driven them away by spoiling them. Or by scaring them! Why not let them be free to do what they want?" Maybe it was the effect of the whisky or whatever, but I added firmly: "Let go of them. The whole lot. And the house too!" But he was hardly listening and the photographs in his pocket-book had appeared again.

Sometimes all manifestations of human anxiety seem very similar to me – at least the everyday matters that people continue to worry about when, so to speak, rain is no longer coming in through the roof, there is no shortage of food and no one is being physically threat-ened – if you understand what I mean. Over and above factual catastrophes, miseries of one sort or another seem to repeat themselves with rather monotonous regularity so far as I've noticed: he or she is unfaithful or bored, someone's no longer enjoying their work, ambitions or dreams have gone out of shape, time's rapidly getting shorter, one's family is behaving in an incomprehensible and frightening way, a friendship has been totally poisoned by something trivial. One is frantically busy with inessentials, while what is important and irreparable goes from bad to worse, duty and blame nibble away at us and the whole syndrome is vaguely labelled angst, a spiritual malaise one seldom succeeds in defining or even tries to define. I know. One's opportunities for feeling ill at ease in life are countless and I recognise them, they constantly return, each affliction in its own little compartment. I should be familiar with this state of affairs and by now I should have found the right answer to the problem but I haven't. There is no practical answer, is there? So we just listen. And anyway, it seems no one is really interested in practical solutions; they just go on talking, they come back and talk about the same thing again and again, they won't let you go. And here I was now sitting with Mr Connaugh, desperately trying not to feel sorry for him. It was going to be rather a long journey. At that particular moment he was holding forth about his misunderstood childhood.

The boat had begun to roll, but not too badly. I never get seasick, but I announced very clearly: "Mr Connaugh, I don't feel very well." "Not Mr Connaugh," he said, "Albert. Didn't I say you should call me Albert? Well, that angst I was talking about..."

"Albert, I'm afraid I'm going to have to go up on deck. I need a little air, I'm not feeling well."

"No problem," he said. "What you need is a straight whisky now – instantly. And you can have all the air you want." He attacked our window, you know the sort of cabin window they screw down firmly with goodness knows what kind of screw apparatus, but he got it open and a violent and extremely wet rush of ice-cold air took my breath away and blew the curtains horizontal while my glass fell to the floor. "Not bad," he said, much revived himself. "I've fixed it. Did you know I once dreamed of being a boxer? Now you'll feel better."

I reached for my overcoat.

"Albert," I said, "what is it you actually do?"

"Business," he answered shortly. My question had clearly depressed him again. There was a long silence. We raised our glasses to each other. Every now and then, salt spray drenched the table. I tried to say something funny about getting extra water in our drinks but it fell flat. To my horror I noticed Mr Connaugh's eyes were full of tears and his face was distorted. "You don't know," he said. "You don't know how it feels..."

It's when they start crying that I'm done for. I promise them anything – my friendship for life, money (though naturally not in this case), my bed, to undertake the most disagreeable tasks, and if it's a big strong man who's weeping... I get desperate. I leaped up and proposed God knows what, the nightclub, the swimming pool, anything, but the boat rolled, making me lose my balance so that I was flung violently against Mr Connaugh. He grabbed me like a drowning man and leaned his great head on my shoulder. It was terrible. From many points of view my position was extremely awkward. I've never known anything like it. Luckily the boat gave an enormous lurch at that moment and a lot of water came in throught the window. Moving with lightning speed, Mr Connaugh rescued his bottle and set about screwing down the window as best he could. I rushed out into the corridor and escaped into blind flight through the bewildering open spaces of the boat.

When I eventually stopped, utterly exhausted, I was almost alone and it was completely silent. I looked in through an open door. Deck-places. Of course, a large room full of low chairs, most of them already tipped backwards for the night. A large number of deck-passengers lying asleep rolled in blankets. I went in, very carefully picked up a spare blanket and chose a chair as far off as possible, against the wall. Wonderful. To be able to sleep and sink into silence, oblivious of everything... I'd developed a terrible headache and I was very wet, but that was nothing, nothing at all. I pulled the blanket over my head and vanished into a total disinterested peace.

When I woke I had no idea where I was. Someone was trying to pull the blanket off me and kept saying that it was her chair, it was number thirty-one and it was her chair and she had a ticket to prove it... I sat up, dazed and confused, and began saying, "Excuse me, I mean it was a misunderstanding and the lighting's so bad, I really am very sorry..." "Don't mention it," said the woman sourly, "I'm used to misunderstandings, that's exactly what they're always called."

My headache had got even worse and I was freezing cold. As far as I could see, nearly all the chairs were already occupied by sleeping people, so I just sat down on the floor and tried to massage my neck. "Haven't you got a ticket?" asked the woman severely.

"No."

"Have you lost it? This part of the boat's full too."

I said nothing. Perhaps they'd let me sleep on the floor.

"Why are you wet?" she asked. "You smell of whisky. My son Herbert drinks whisky. Once he fell in the lake."

She sat and watched me with my blanket up under my chin. She was a bony little grey-haired woman, tanned and with small sharp eyes. She'd put her hat at her feet. She went on: "My suitcase is over there. Please bring it here if you can. It's best to have your things close beside you in a place like this. Mind the cake-box. That's for Herbert."

Afterwards, more people came in, looking for their chairs. The boat was rolling violently and not far off someone was being sick into a bag.

"It'll be different in London," said the old woman, pulling her suitcase nearer. "I just need to find out where Herbert is right now. D'you know where you have to go to find out people's addresses?" "No," I said. "But perhaps the purser..."

"Are you going to sleep on the floor all night?"

"Yes. I'm very tired."

"I can understand." She added: "Whisky's expensive." And a little later: "Have you got any food in you?"

"No. I thought as much. There was food in the grill. But it was too expensive for me."

I huddled on the floor, buttoned up my overcoat and tried to sleep. It didn't work. How could this person go all the way to London without even knowing her son's address? And they'd be sure to stop her when she landed; these days you had to give references and prove you had enough money before they'd let you in... Where was she from? Somewhere in the country... She'd baked a cake for that son of hers... My God, how helpless and unpractical can you get!

I slept for a bit and woke again. She was snoring and had thrown an arm over the edge of the chair, her hand looked tired, a wrinkled brown hand with broad wedding and engagement rings. Now lots of people were being sick here and there round the room and the stench was frightful. I decided to go up on deck. My old dislike of lifts came over me at that moment, so I went up the stairs and passed the grill. People were still sitting and eating there. I hesitated a moment, then bought several large sandwiches and a bottle of beer and went back down the stairs and managed to find the place I'd just come from. She was awake.

"No, but that really was so kind of you," she said and immediately attacked the sandwiches, "won't you have half?" But I wasn't hungry any more, and sat thinking about how much money she might need to be allowed to land. Wasn't there some sort of Christian hostel that looked after confused travellers? I must find the purser, perhaps he would know...

"My name's Emma Fagerberg," she said.

The person lying on the next chair emerged from under a blanket and said: "Shut up! I'm trying to sleep."

She pulled out her handbag from under her pillow. "You've been so kind," whispered Mrs Emma Fagerberg. "I'll show you some photos of my son. This is what Herbert looked like when he was four. The picture's a little blurred, but I have several others which are much better... "

Taking Leave

THERE CAME A SUMMER WHEN IT WAS SUDDENLY AN effort to pull in the nets. The terrain became unmanageable and treacherous. This made us more surprised than alarmed, perhaps we weren't old enough yet, but to be on the safe side I built a couple of steps and Tooti fixed up some guide ropes and hand grips here and there, and we continued as usual but ate less fish.

It got worse: for example, when I no longer felt like going up on the roof to sweep the chimney (and made the excuse that I wanted to work, believe it or not). And that last summer something unforgivable happened: I became afraid of the sea. Large waves were no longer connected with adventure, only anxiety and responsibility for the boat, and indeed all boats that ply the sea in bad weather. It wasn't fair; even in my worst dreams the sea had always been an unfailing deliverance: the danger was after you, but you hopped in and sailed away and were safe and never returned. That fear felt like a betrayal – my own.

Gradually we invented a secret game that involved making the objects change place. We imagined where these things, these too long-respected treasures, might be allowed to, as it were, wake up after their sleep – whether they had been inherited, captured or found on the shore. Among the finest of them, perhaps, were a door panel with 'Captain's Cabin' in brass, grandfather's barometer and a mate's certificate washed up by the tide.

We had century-old net-floats with owners' marks and sinkers tied up in birch bark and elegant lettering from the finely dovetailed wooden crates that bobbed up on the beaches now and then – Napoleon Cognac, Old Smuggler's Whisky, oranges from Jamaica and also a few items we had been given by well-meaning folk, such as a ship's log, a half-sextant and an enormous block from a ketch. Now all these more or less esteemed items were to be given to other islands where people still had enough of the pioneer in them to turn their houses into maritime museums.

We knew that now it was time to give the house away. We assured each other that it was more stylish to leave in time, before one was forced to, but this got a bit tedious if one said it too often.

I sat down and wrote that there is a fine balance between the absolute calm of arrival and the excitement of departure, then crossed out 'fine' and added 'both are indispensable' at the end, and began to wonder what I had really meant.

Gradually we began to put up small, helpful pieces of paper here and there, such as 'Don't close the damper; it rusts and sticks', 'The key is by the door-post', or 'Woollen stockings and socks under the boot rack', and so on. Certain objects had to be explained, for no one could be expected to know that an excrement-yellow lump weighing five kilos was seal fat for the preparation of the wooden jetty.

"How to get to the secret room?" I said, but Tooti considered that they could find it themselves, and one should not underestimate their natural curiosity. All the same, we put a small bottle of rum in there as a surprise and a reward.

It may be noted that in the winter Tooti's secret room contained fifty pistol cartridges, three sparking plugs, Ham's* best bark boat, the tools for the Honda, the barometer and father's statuette.

Tooti loves packing because she is so good at it. In former years, every time spring drew near she began to pack for the island as early as February, slightly embarrassed at her joyful haste. I suppose I knew what was up when, first of all, she oiled Becker's little copperplate press and its rollers with Evergrease. On her list there were usually notes for Sangajol, Swarfega, turpentine and cotton waste, among other things. I knew it: after

* Ham – Tove's mother, the artist Signe Hammarsten Jansson.

professional matters came tools, then books and music, then all the other things, such as:

Blacking, Caramba
Gun oil and lead subacetate
Girls' Cookery Book and Book of Handy Hints
Emergency pistol
Shackle for Victoria + 25,30
Fishing line no. 26, 23, 20, 80cm
Sail rings, hooks
Copper nails, 2 fish chests (for the cat)
20kg apples
Stone wax
Mantles for Aladdin lamp
Teak oil + 5 litres olive oil
Norwegian thermal wear
Seed potatoes
Gas cylinders 5 and 10 litres, radio batteries
Hinges for cellar hatch
Gearbox lubricant and Sinol

After that came all the food.

Those lists were very useful from one spring to the next, for one forgets more and more things during the winter. Now Tooti was packing for the city. We didn't talk about it much. The weather stayed fine.

One morning I took in the nets that were to be hung away in the cellar and suddenly reflected that I would never need to fish again. I went down to the old sawing-place in the ravine. The wild rose bushes there had grown so enormously that there was not much of the woodshed to be seen. All the same, I went and sat down under the cupola in order to think.

So I never had to fish again. Never again throw the slops into the sea or be afraid about rainwater, never again suffer agonies over *Victoria* and the fact that no one, no one, had any need to concern themselves with us! Good. Then I began to think: why can't a meadow be allowed to run wild in peace and quiet, and why can't the pretty stones be allowed to tumble down as they want to without being admired, and so on, and gradually I got angry and thought that the cruel bird war could look after itself and as far as I was concerned any damned gull that liked was welcome to suppose that it owned the whole house!

I went home again and began a list, 'Reasons For Not Living On An Island', and Tooti looked in and said: "Are you writing? If it's about *Victoria's* shipwreck – but don't be hurt now…"

"Alright, tell me," I said.

"Well, if you could try to be a little objective for once. Don't set the gale on an autumn night, but tell it the way it was: it came in the middle of the day, in the middle of summer, on 15 July 1991. Report that it was 9 on the Beaufort scale, 20–24 metres per second, south-easterly, of course. And write it in the present tense, which makes it seem more dramatic. Like this, for example: the sea rises violently, turning black and speckled, the house gives a shudder, and then it's all over."

I said: "How about 'the birds are silent'?"

"That's alright," said Tooti, "but anyhow, *Victoria* is taken by surprise, there are assaults from every side, backwash from the stern, water over the prow, she fights bravely on her four ropes – write that I fitted new ones every spring – and all her shackles. Say that now the sea is coming in over the stern thwart, just a little splash, and then another little splash, but it goes on and on! Draw it out as long as you can."

I knew. Tooti stood on watch at the north window all night; sometimes she would pop below to check that the ropes were slack, then just go on standing. I think that at those times she talked to the boat.

"Continue," said Tooti. "Write that at ten past four *Victoria* filled with water to the gunwale and sank, slowly and nobly. Write that at eight o'clock I made contact with Pellinge on our newly installed radio telephone. I report, very calmly, that now it has happened and they think it's you who have tumbled down the rock, but I say: '*Victoria* has been wrecked.' They bestir themselves and set out at once to see what's up, but can't even contemplate putting to land in that heavy sea, so we just wave to one another. Nonetheless, they come out once again…"

I interrupted her and said wasn't it getting a bit too long, but Tooti went on: "They come out a second time and now they have two sea captains and a pilot aboard. The sea has gone down just enough so they can lift *Victoria* out of the water and haul her to land by her stern ropes and she glides along on her ropes, undamaged. Imagine that: glides exactly midway between the

rocks and the gale and doesn't lose anything but her forward grating and the Yamaha battery! Write that I started up the Yamaha just for the good of the cause and that it ran for almost ten minutes! And that I'd stowed the oars below the thwart so they were still there."

That year, quite late in the autumn, Brunstrom came by. He promised to look after Uncle Torsten's nets, some four-inch planks and half a sack of cement.

"So you'll leave," he said. "Anyone can see there's not much spare stuff left round here any more."

He made a tour around the house in order to make sure that everything was in order and we followed after. The water butts were turned upside down in the proper fashion and secured so they would not blow away, the window shutters ready to be closed with hasps, and various items prepared for the approaching winter.

Brunstrom thought we had left it all very cosy and even inhabitable, though the veranda planks could do with a coating, in view of the snow that was to come. He said: "And now we'll go and take a look at another kind of island I doubt you ever thought of."

It was dead calm. Brunstrom steered straight to the south, quite a long distance. He put in at an islet that was very high and steep, formed from three round-worn rocks close together. Between them plunged deep fissures, in which the water ceaselessly rose and fell, even though the sea was completely still. The islet was made of black rock, not like our part of the world.

Brunstrom waited in the boat, for there was nowhere to moor.

"Well, what do you think?" he said. "Not a blade of grass grows here; there's nothing and nothing, and in a way I think that's precisely the beauty of it."

Tooti wanted to know what the islet was called, but it had no name. When we got home the timber was loaded into Brunstrom's boat and we got on with coating the veranda planks with tar because the Valtii impregnant was finished.

On the last day, when Tooti was clearing up the cellar, she found one of our kites from the 1960s and took it out onto the slope. Just for fun, she gave it a little push on its tail and at that moment a gust of wind came along and took the kite with it and it flew high, straight up, and continued far out across the Gulf of Finland.

Afterwords

Philip Pullman

Tove Jansson was a rare and extraordinary writer: a being seemingly composed equally of woman, nature spirit, sea creature and Moomin, whose consciousness was both exquisitely local (the famous island where she lived every summer) and generously universal (her understanding of all the processes of life and the passage of time).

These stories show a side of her that may be new to some British readers, who perhaps think of her, if at all, as a writer of charming stories for children. They are as tough as good rope, these stories, as smooth and odd and beautiful as sea-worn driftwood, as full of light and air and wind as the Nordic summer. We are lucky to have them collected at last.

Esther Freud

These stories are infused with such a strong sense of Tove
Jansson's character that by the last page you feel on almost
intimate terms with her. Determined, indignant, fearless, as a child,
we see how she develops – have the luxury of glimpsing her as
an old lady too, still determined, still indignant, so that it is with a
shock that we catch her – for both her and us – in a rare moment
of fear. But what never changes about Tove Jansson is her passion
for nature, her love of the bleak rocks and shrieking gulls of the
Pelinge peninsular and, above all, the sea. As a young girl she
disobeys her father and rows out into a rough sea by moonlight
'all splinters and flakes from precious stones like sailing through
a sea set with diamonds', and many years later we recognise
the same stubborn core of the woman who declares war on a
squirrel, the only other inhabitant of her island home.

Frank Cottrell Boyce

As a child I knew all there was to know about the world Tove
Jansson created – the Moominvalley and the Lonely Mountains
– but nothing whatsoever about her. I never saw a picture of her,
had no idea if she was alive, dead, male or female. So meeting
the real Tove in these stories has been an exciting and unnerving
experience – a bit like meeting my own guardian angel.

Luckily Tove seems to have been all that a guardian angel
should be – wise, stern and flighty. Like an angel, she thinks
that humans are funny and vulnerable – tiny creatures busily
accumulating grandeur and clutter on the surface of a dangerous

and unpredictable planet. In an era when the weather seems to be going haywire, this is an exhilaratingly prescient vision.

But she also has a strong sense that, if we're kind to each other, and if we take the time to learn to how to do things properly – if we make sure there's enough firewood, and that the roof doesn't leak – then somehow it will all be alright and possibly fun.

My favourite story here is 'The Iceberg'. A little girl sees an iceberg and dreams of riding away on it. The iceberg comes within her reach but, instead of jumping on board, she only wedges her torch in a little grotto at its base and watches it float away, illuminated now with a new inner light, like a great floating emerald. She does not go out and conquer the wilderness. She does not return home with trophies of antlers or wild flowers. She gives away something of herself and somehow gains. And obviously, being Tove, she makes sure the torch has fresh batteries.

I'm very glad I set such store by Tove Jansson as a child. She's been a good guardian angel to me.